ever re...
always does'
Nick Lezard, *Guardia*...

*

For *The Oxford Despoiler*

'Wonderful ... stuffed with period detail, literary gags
and cameo parts (including a monosyllabic Oscar
Wilde). The whole thing is a delight'
Sunday Telegraph

'Grossly entertaining. Smutty, silly, very funny, and
definitely not breakfast-table reading'
Observer

'Deliciously silly, but crafted with such wry histor-
ical precision that Conan Doyle himself would
struggle to deduce he was a parody'
Time Out

'Sheer comic genius'
Michael Bywater

NATURAL
DESIRE IN
HEALTHY
WOMEN

First published in 2014 by Old Street Publishing Ltd,

www.oldstreetpublishing.co.uk

ISBN 978 1 908699 41 1

Copyright © Gary Dexter, 2014

10 9 8 7 6 5 4 3 2 1

A CIP catalogue record for this title is available from the
British Library.

Printed and bound by CPI Group (UK) Ltd, Croydon, CR0 4YY

NATURAL DESIRE IN HEALTHY WOMEN

GARY
DEXTER

ALSO BY GARY DEXTER

Why Not Catch-21?
Title Deeds
The Oxford Despoiler (and other mysteries from the casebook of Henry St. Liver)
All the Materials for a Midnight Feast

NOTE FROM THE AUTHOR

This book is based on the life of the birth control campaigner Marie Stopes (1880-1958), who did or said hardly any of the things in these pages.

Unto the pure all things are pure: but unto them that are defiled and unbelieving is nothing pure; but even their mind and conscience is defiled.

Titus 1:15

CONTENTS

PART TWO

PART ONE

THE BEGINNING

On the morning of 2nd September H.G. tele-phoned with some news.

'I suppose you've seen the *Express*,' he said.

'I never read the *Express*.'

'There's an Australian fellow who claims that you pose the greatest threat to the Empire since the rise of Bolshevism and that you must be destroyed.'

'Who?' I asked.

'Some politician or other. The Prime Minister, I think.'

'Why?'

'I imagine the usual reasons.'

But the true answer came in a flash. The Aboriginal tribespeople, who had not yet heard of the benefits of the 'Racial' sponge and simple vegetable oil, or alternatively the 'Pro-Race' high-dome rubber check pessary, were reproducing at a rapid rate, and the white inhabitants of Melbourne and Sydney, restricted to the fringes of their continent, were finding themselves unable to control the feckless breeding of the central mass... a race of intellectually and physically stunted resentful Aboriginal malcontents.

But to demonise *me*, when only I offer the solution!

'And I need your advice,' H.G. went on. 'Last night the spheres returned. Glittering green spheres, amid the trees, moving gently and sighing.'

'Apples,' I said, putting the telephone down slowly. 'They are apple trees.'

It seemed that the Catholic Church and its minions were gaining in influence. This recent attack from Australia could only have been masterminded from Rome. An attempt – ultimately successful – had already been made to burn down my travelling birth-control caravan in Birmingham, and by one of the very nurses who was supposed to be staffing it! After consuming two bottles of gin, she had ignited some gauze with a cigar.

And only that year, 1925, there had been the Papal Encyclical *Casti Connubii*, which, as anyone with an ounce of sense could see, was aimed squarely at me:

> The Church of Christ, rising erect from the moral ruin which surrounds her, condemns utterly the practice of preventing the conception of children. The infant Christ would weep to see these iniquities, which arise from the perverted desire to frustrate God's design for humanity. Eternal punishment – in one of the lower circles of hell, not in one of the comparatively tolerable ones around the fringes where pagan philosophers go – awaits those who persist in this work of Lucifer.

It was time for a new campaign.

MARGARET, AND THE OBTUSENESS OF A WAITRESS

I am proud to say that I was a formative influence on the work of Margaret Sanger. For years I exchanged letters with dear Margaret across the Atlantic, but our first face-to-face meeting was in April 1921, at a small corner-restaurant in Aldwych, The Golden Egg. It was undoubtedly what led her to her present success.

I remember my first glimpse of her. She was sitting at a table underneath a chandelier, and on her head was an enormous hat which trailed red and green feathers. Even seated she looked like a giantess. As I approached her table our eyes met, disconcertingly, at the same level.

'Amber! Sit by me, lovely one!' she boomed, patting the bench next to her.

I did so, and at the same moment a waitress arrived. Margaret asked for steak and onions. When told that the bill of fare comprised mainly teas, pastries and light meals, she evinced some disappointment, but eventually ordered three bacon rolls and a cup of coffee. I decided on tea and a macaroon.

'That is the model of downtrodden womanhood in this country,' Margaret said, none too quietly, gesturing after the waitress.

'She did look a little tired.'

'You saw the band on her finger? An engagement ring. Soon her Prince Charming will take her from here to a Palace of Labour that will make this seem like a rest home. Year after year the children will accumulate, each one with less and less strength, each one with less and less intellectual capacity – less even than their mother, who has never heard of steak and onions. In a decade she will be worn out. And all because she has no knowledge of family limitation.'

'In Britain we have made *some* strides in that direction, I like to think, although there is of course much yet to achieve,' I said. 'My book *Wedded Love…*'

'Dear, I have read your book. It is excellent, of course. But surely wedded love is half the problem. I am willing to wager that poor creature knows nothing even of the rudiments of reproduction.'

'It is possible,' I admitted.

At that moment the waitress returned to the table.

'Sorry, cook says there's no bacon.'

There was a pause. 'No bacon,' echoed Margaret, nodding ominously. Then she fixed the waitress with a bright smile. 'May I ask, dear – I do hope you don't mind my asking – have you given any thought to prevention?'

'Beg pardon, Ma'am?'

'I really have no wish to embarrass you – please tell me if you would prefer not to answer – but I and my friend here are poised on the edge of a campaign to liberate women from slavery. So my question was, in regard to your future married state – and again, I beg you not to answer if you find a particle of embarrassment in it – do you favour the sheath?'

I gathered from this that Margaret's own preference was for the sheath, so I awaited the response with interest.

'Do you mean Rudolf Valentino?'

'No, no, dear, the *sheath*. Look, I have one here.' Margaret reached into a large black medical bag, and laid on the table a flabby rubber tube which looked as if it had already been used. At the time I doubted that such could have been the case.

The waitress looked at the object and then at Margaret, and then at the feathers in Margaret's hat. She seemed unwilling or unable to reply.

'As I suspected,' said Margaret. 'The simple condom. Unknown.'

'My colleague wished only to enquire,' I said soothingly to the girl, 'whether you had any intention of using the device. Of course I quite understand your feelings.' I reached into my own more modest receptacle, where I had a good supply of 'Racial' rubber sponges. The device had at the time not received its world monomark, so I was cognisant of the risk I was taking in exposing it to the full view of my American rival. 'I share the concern that the sheath does not allow the healthful interpenetration of secretions.'

'That is Schrenk-Notzing's view, certainly,' said Margaret coolly.

'And mine.'

'I don't doubt it,' said Margaret. She turned her eyes to the girl. 'Well then, perhaps *this* is more in your line.' With a rapid jerk of the arm she produced a huge rubber diaphragm, which she must have been holding at the ready in her lap. The appearance of this object made the waitress start back. It looked like a marine creature. There was a noticeable diminution of background noise in The Golden Egg.

'What is it?' the waitress asked fearfully.

'It is the Mensinga cap,' declared Margaret. 'It has been used with complete success in Holland for almost a generation, and yet no British woman has ever seen one.'

'I have seen one,' I countered, 'and I believe it stretches the vagina. I would invite you to compare the sponge. You see, dear,' I said confidentially to the waitress, 'it can be used with ordinary vegetable oil, a condiment to be found in any kitchen.'

I had expected the waitress to brighten at the mention of kitchens, but her small eyes remained fixed in horror on Margaret's jellyfish. Nevertheless I went on: 'And so, for that matter, can this.'

I gracefully unfolded my hand, where I had concealed what I felt would be the 'stinger'.

'The high-domed solid-rim cervical cap, size one,' I said with quiet dignity, remarking with satisfaction the contrast with the jellyfish. 'What do you say to that?'

'Is it for babies?' the girl asked.

'Quite the contrary,' I said. 'It is a contraceptive device.' The blank expression on the waitress's face suggested that further explanation was needed. 'To insert the cap,' I continued, 'you simply need to find a comfortable position, perhaps standing with one foot raised on a stool, or lying down with knees bent, and then, using the fingers of one hand to create the required aperture, you squeeze the rim of the cap with your other hand…' ('No, no, no,' muttered my luncheon partner) '…and push it over your cervix. You can run your finger around the rim of the cap to make sure that the cervix is covered. See how the suction works on this pool of coffee,' I ventured somewhat teasingly, 'although it should of course be washed afterwards. 'Go on, try it. Test the suction by gently pinching and pulling on it. You should feel some resistance.'

At this point a little, greasy man appeared at the table: to judge from his dress and demeanour, he was an off-duty poulterer. He was very red in the face.

'Now thass enough of that,' he huffed. 'You oughter be ashamed, talking like that to this young lady. She don't understand but I do. I'll fetch a policeman.'

'I beg your pardon,' said Margaret, rising from her seat. There was a great deal of her. The feathers on her hat brushed the chandelier, making it jingle. She was seven feet tall if she was an inch. The colour departed from the man's face.

'Is it your contention,' Margaret said loudly, speaking ostensibly to him, but in reality addressing The Golden Egg in general, 'that there are parts of the human body that may not be mentioned in a Christian restaurant in this country? Why do you not liberate yourselves and your children from mental bondage?'

'I'll give you mental bondage,' parried the man. 'I said I'd fetch a policeman and I will.' He tried to make good his escape, but was unable to, for the reason that Margaret now had him firmly by the arm.

'Woman is a creature of whim and fancy,' she brayed. 'As much as any man, she has a right to erotic fulfillment. And yet, for her, the consequences of her sex-yearning are to be tormented by the very body that has given her such delight. Imprisonment, pain, punishment! In this very capital thousands of women die every year in childbirth! Thousands more babies are born unloved and uncared for!'

'You let go!'

'Women of The Golden Egg!' Margaret shouted. 'In you is the single miraculous fertilisation that brings life into being! But may you be spared the long-drawn-out nightmare of an *unwanted* embryo growing within you – the most intimate and insidious of horrors!'

With that she raised her left hand in rhetorical appeal; it was still holding the jellyfish, which flapped. Several cries of insidious horror did indeed go up. Simultaneously Margaret let go the little man, who was so eager to escape that it seemed more as if she had propelled him down the aisle. Skittering on his heels, he span and fell on a trolley containing cakes and hot water. There was a loud crash and some screaming.

'Dear Margaret,' I said. 'How about the British Library? Perhaps we could continue our discussion there.'

'Very well,' Margaret pronounced after a pause, eyeing the scene of devastation. 'Intellectual refreshment will have to take the place of bodily refreshment. Lead on, lovely one!'

Margaret, I believe, learned much from this

encounter. The essential contact had been made. It was not long after her return to the United States, following our meeting, that the Comstock obscenity laws were repealed, allowing the free flow of contraceptive information through the mails. I often heard subsequently of her campaigning successes and public appearances in Europe and America. Her methods were of course quite damaging and wrong, and her pronouncements concerning the sanctity of the working class and so on utterly false, and we pursued our separate ways and did not exchange a word for four years. But on the day I received that telephone call from H.G., I decided that Margaret would be the first person to learn of my new campaign.

Consequently I sat down in the little office at Westbury and dictated to my Secretary Number Two as follows:

2 September 1925
Westbury Park, nr Dorking

Dear Margaret,

How time has flown since we last spoke! There has been all the triumph of my three trials, the most recent before the House of Lords, and the resulting demand for my books, and I have had barely time to draw breath, so I apologise for not writing sooner. Attacks from the established churches have grown in virulence. The Irish Censorship Bill has meant that none of the newspapers in Eire are permitted to carry advertisements for rubber goods. Only today I received a letter from the *Catholic Herald* stating that it was regrettably unable to publish an article I had submitted on the topic of the Inquisition. The Catholic Church has a stranglehold on men's minds. I have been forced to take ever more drastic steps in response, such as chaining copies of my books to railings outside Westminster Cathedral.

Despite all this, or because of it, I have decided to undertake a new publishing project – a periodical. It will contain news, opinion and, most prominently, extended essays by leading thinkers on the topics of birth control and eugenics. I intend to canvass not only the world's great campaigners and scientists, but also our most eminent poets and artists. The aim will be nothing less than to smash organised religion. For the first time, ordinary men and women will be able to hear the true teaching of Jesus Christ, who preached only a normal, natural and healthy attitude towards sex life.

Please let me know whether you would be interested in contributing to such a project. How is Freddie? Is he still wearing the knitted woollen trousers we discussed?

I look forward so much to hearing from you.

Yours ever,

Amber Haldane

Little did I know that in twelve months' time, as a direct result, I would be a guest on a small island in the Setonaikai Sea.

WEDDED LOVE

Wedded Love, on its publication in 1918, had much the same impact on the world as a man falling on a cake-trolley generally has in a crowded tea house. That is to say, pandemonium. I was both extolled and excoriated. Accusations of immorality were perhaps the most frequent line of attack, but my detractors also made play with my supposed desire for self-enrichment and self-aggrandisement, my insensitivity in the face of war losses, my defective taste, wish to destroy the Empire, blasphemy, medical inaccuracy, hubris, insanity and eugenic over-enthusiasm, often by the same post.

Running counter to this bitter torrent, however, was another, greater flood: of love. Women and men of all races, ages and creeds wrote to me expressing support for my work. Many women invited me into their homes to gather material for my next book. I soon had to hire a large team of secretaries merely to keep up with the post I received. Personal replies were soon out of the question – it was enough work simply to insert a form-letter dealing with the most common problems. My publisher, Fifield, bore the brunt of the avalanche of mail, and complained bitterly that, one way or another, *Wedded Love* had taken over the entire business. On an average day he would receive 160 bags of mail, filled to bursting – each bag the size of a person of small to medium height[1]. Soon he no longer had room for anything else, and yet it was imperative that he hire new staff to keep *Wedded Love* (which had broken all records for the firm) rolling off the presses.

Still the letters arrived. I calculated that if every man, woman and child in Britain had written a letter to me about their sex difficulties, it would still not have accounted for the prodigious volume of correspondence I received. Finally I realised that the secretaries I had employed at Westbury were posting their replies back to the publisher to be forwarded on to the correspondents, but that the publisher was returning them as if they were new letters. My secretaries duly treated these in the same way, inserting a form-letter and posting them back once more, thus creating an endless cycle. Unfortunately by the time I had arrived at this crucial insight, Fifield had blown his brains out with his service pistol. Undeterred, I sought a new publisher. I urgently needed to recoup my losses, having spent £3,267 6s 4d on postage.

Judging by the tenor of a good 43 per cent of my postbag, religious questions were a common thread of preoccupation, particularly the writings of the Apostle Paul and the more minatory sections of the Book of Revelation. It struck me that the support of the Church of England would be of enormous importance in swaying the public mood in favour of contraceptive rights. I determined, therefore, to create a questionnaire that could be sent out to 5,000 vicars selected at random from *Crockford's*.

---

1 Or perhaps a large dwarf.

This, it seemed to me, would bring me closer to the heart of Church thinking.

The questionnaire was as follows:

STRICTLY PRIVATE & CONFIDENTIAL

To be returned to Dr Amber Haldane, Westbury Park, near Dorking, Surrey.

The information requested is asked in the interests of biological and anthropological research on the needs of married people. It has been addressed to Anglican clergymen alone, on the presumption that they will be more amenable to argument and persuasion, and will be better able to provide a representative picture of how rational beings go about sex activity. The more explicit the replies the better. No names will ever be divulged, used in diaries, autobiographies, or mentioned casually in the presence of anyone of any religious stamp or denomination whatsoever, or atheists or pantheists, or indeed anyone at all; the information will be treated with complete scientific detachment and tabulated in an emotionless manner. It will emphatically NOT be deposited with the British Library on open access.

Please state:
    1) The number of years married
    2) The age of wife
    3) The condition of wife
    4) The age of wife at first parturition
    5) The number of children born, including miscarriages and stillbirths

6) Which children seem the most promising, eugenically speaking

7) Whether any methods of preventing undue increase of the family have been adopted

8) If such means have been adopted, whether any of the following were used:

(i) Total abstention (state how many years or decades)

(ii) Limitation of unions to safe periods

(iii) Limitation of unions to weekends or public holidays, or non-Lenten periods

(iv) Use of withdrawal – i.e. *coitus interruptus*

(v) Use of pessary

(vi) Use of Mensinga cap (not recommended)

(vii) Use of 'Racial' rubber sponge and solvent

(viii) Use of cervical cap of any of the following types:

(a) hollow-rim

(b) high-domed solid rim

(c) self-cleaning

(d) numbers 1–3

(e) numbers 4–6

(f) numbers 7–35*

(ix) Use of sheath

(x) Use of quinine

(xi) Use of zinc

(xii) Use of alum

(xiii) Use of ergot

(xiv) Use of boron

(xv) Jumping, bouncing, etc. after coitus

(xvi) Standing up

(xvii) Sealing the navel with sticking plaster

(xviii) Not touching the breasts during intercourse

(xix) Opposite corners of the room

(xx) Prayer

(xxi) Other means

9) Any particulars of individual sex peculiarities

10) Notable individual experiences presented in a narrative form.

Signed _____

Date_____

Address_____

_____

_____

This form may be sent back anonymously if required.

* If over size 35, state why.

The responses confirmed my suspicions that Anglicanism would present a 'broad Church' indeed on these matters. Some respondents assumed that contraception was forbidden by the Church, and eschewed it as zealously as any Papist. Most seemed never to have heard of the majority of the techniques I mentioned. A small number had experimented with methods such as zinc, which, when used directly on the genitals in its granular form, acts as a powerful anti-aphrodisiac.

Outright abstention was very commonly encountered as a contraceptive method, as was the strict avoidance of any stimulation likely to lead to female orgasm.

There was much forthright comment on the issues I had raised. Some representative responses I set down here.

'I blame you for the Great War. If there is ever another comparable conflagration I blame you for that too. You are a monster.'
Revd E. H. Badger

'God bless you, you are a beacon to this country and a blessing to mankind.'
Mrs Ruth Hale, Blakeney Post Office
(opened in error)

'So many lads during the war acquired the habit of self-pollution. I read in one of your books while at the front that relaxing in a large, warm, steaming bath (the hotter the better) was an infallible cure but could never find adequate facilities to test the theory.'
Revd Bertie 'BB' Butler

'Thou shalt do no murder... If God sends the babies he sends their breeches.'
Revd Rupert Mancroft

'What abominably impudent questions!'
Mrs Revd Rupert Mancroft

'We second what mother and father have said.'

Anna, Abigail, Arthur, Alan, Adalbert,
Avelina and Absalom Mancroft

'Dear noted bogus doctor of German philosophy Mrs Haldane, you are nothing but a pornographer; your books are textbooks of practical prostitution. I consider your questionnaire absolutely criminal. Nothing doing.'

Revd Elisha Bigg-Wither

'I am glad that you raise eugenic concerns. The lower orders, if allowed to breed unchecked, could, by very pressure of numbers, rise and be a danger to the community. I think the time is not very far distant when we shall have to consider seriously what we are to do with the insane, the hopeless invalid, and all who are irredeemably degraded in mind and body… A painless extinction seems to be the only remedy, perhaps using some kind of poison gas. Nor do I see anything unchristian in such action.'

Revd A. Jodl

'I suffer from an inflammation of the sensual and animal part of myself which I find overwhelmingly shameful, morally painful and disgusting. Thank you for your interesting books.'

Mr Edwin Dowson

'I have appended a diary in which I have recorded my sex activity.

Monday	Wife away at mother's
Tuesday	ditto
Wednesday	ditto
Thursda	ditto
Friday	ditto
Saturday	ditto; rubbed "matter" out of erect penis by hand
Sunday	Was rubbing "matter" out again when she came back and saw me. I said, "Emily, I was going to tell you but you would never listen. You are never here when you ought to be. I demand that you assist me in this matter." Slowly putting down her basket she came over to me then hesitated and went back to the basket; she got out a fresh loaf, and while I watched cut off two slices.'

Revd J. Bank

'My son has obtained the London Matric. And my daughter plays the piano and oboe and speaks seven languages: English, French, German, Italian, Greek, Hebrew and Ancient Assyrian. The last she learned at age nine just by looking at a book I had on my desk. She has recently made a good marriage with a local abattoir man. The chops we get are very good.'

Revd P. P. Furrier

'I am a bachelor and I have the desire occasionally to produce seed which I have found I can do by hand, although the presence of my middle-aged cook appears to help. Is this normal? I enclose a cheque for any of your books you care to send, since I cannot order from the local bookseller.'

Anon

'Casanova, I believe, recommended a half-lemon.'

Revd S. Woode

'I am a normal married clergyman with a lovely baby boy, about thirty-two years old. I have been unable to carry out coitus for any length of time before being overcome by excitement. I have tried to cure this with long periods of abstention. I withhold union from my wife for a fortnight, as recommended in your book *Wedded Love*, but when I approach her after this time find I am unable to resist spending. I have, with all due deference to your expert knowledge in these matters, tried to prolong abstention still further, to three weeks or even four, before returning to my wife's bedroom. Invariably she is awaiting me in a fever of impatience, but as soon as I pass through the door to the bedroom am on my knees in an agony of shame. Should I try two months, or even three?'

Revd G Minichid

'While in Nyasaland as an Army chaplain, my wife took quinine practically every day, as it was a most malarious district, yet she found herself with child on three occasions.'

Revd Francis Hatch

'My employer commits himself rigorously to once-a-week unions, in the following way: after Evensong on Saturday he asks me to wait upstairs in the bedroom in a state of undress while he remains downstairs. After a while I begin to hear him making noises – at first a low grunting and snuffling which gradually works up into an angry bellowing, stamping, screaming and weeping, in which no English words can be distinguished. At this point he slowly mounts the stairs, all the while pounding on the walls and roaring like a bull, and flings open the door of the bedroom, revealing himself to be wearing an apron and holding a teatray with a fresh pot of tea, flowers and biscuits.'

Housekeeper to Revd X. Minton

'All of my children are colour-blind and ster-ile. It may be pertinent that I have never fed them anything but bacon.'

Revd J. Greenback

'There was no opportunity to consummate union since my wife began having children immediately after our marriage. Further births in rapid succession continued to make it impossible to have a normal sex life. Because of her frequent confinements – seventeen pregnancies in all – I have never touched her in the course of fifteen years.'

Revd Michael Master

'So many, *many* lads have acquired the habit of self-pollution. I thought I'd write again as the problem is becoming urgent. Is there *anything* you could suggest?'

Revd Bertie 'BB' Butler

'I have always heard it said that women cannot conceive if they are breast-feeding, and so make sure my wife is perpetually occupied in this manner by having numerous infants.'

Revd C. Hareplume

'I have further heard it said that women cannot conceive if they do not experience pleasurable sensations during intercourse, and so make sure my wife never enjoys it.'

Revd C. Hareplume (by separate post)

'It is my view that any sort of control over fertility is against Christian doctrine. Abortion can be considered an evil crime, since it deprives an individual of life, but contraception must be considered Satanic, since it removes the chance for life to exist at all. I hope this is of some assistance.'

Revd A. Pollyon

'Women are not passive instruments of male passion. They have their own autonomous sexual drives. I believe in any and all methods of contraception, abortion on demand, and free love between consenting adults regardless of sexual orientation. As far as my own profession is concerned, I see no reason why women, divorced persons, or homosexuals should not be priests. Obviously, I set these views down as a parody of your own position. However, I think that is where your opinions will be leading us in a few years' time.'

Revd M. Sibyl

'I have further heard it said that playing chess during intercourse can prevent conception as long as neither player is prepared to "mate". This is a very good joke I read somewhere.'

Revd C. Hareplume (by separate post)

It seemed that little in the way of support could be expected from the Anglican Church.

DR ELLIS

Within a few weeks of my contacting her, Margaret wrote to say that she would be delighted to contribute to my new periodical. I had another small success too, in the person of H.G. himself, who, when I telephoned him and told him of his part in prompting the initiative, insisted on writing a piece for the first issue. He was, he admitted, rather burdened with work: recent days had seen the publication of his book *What Must Be Done Now*, a study of, among other things, the German question, proportional representation, rocket travel, free milk, land ironclads, John Galsworthy, immigration, emigration, giant ants and Good Education for All, and in fact a sequel, *What Then Must We Do?*, dealing with, *inter alia*, the restoration of Palestine to the Jews, worker's conferences and the prospect of colonies on Venus was due the following week, and he had only written a third of it. Nevertheless, he was certain he could produce something.

'How are the apples?' I asked.

'Your insight was correct in a sense,' he replied. 'And yet what is more mysterious than an apple?'

I did not pursue the matter, not wishing to provoke him into devoting further time and energy to it.

'However,' H.G. went on, 'I do need your advice. Today I was at Gurling House at a meeting chaired by Sydney Webb on the subject of the Third, or possibly Fourth, International. Bennett, O'Connor and Shaw were there, and we were just about to break for tea. I glanced out of the window. Rolling toward the house was a vast furry thing, green, fifty feet high. My first thought was that it must be some sort of super-conscious entity.'

'A hill,' I said, putting the telephone down slowly. 'Gurling House is at the foot of a hill.'

One began to doubt whether H.G. would produce anything coherent at all on the subject of birth control or eugenics, although his capacity for sheer hard work is startling. In 1924 he claimed to have written over 300 books, including the best-selling *The Day the World Went Whoooossh*. Admittedly these are all rather vulgar productions, but H.G. counters that he regularly attends the opera and knows Mr E.M. Forster personally (though not too personally).

My next scalp was altogether more impressive: that of Dr Henry Havelock Ellis.

For some time I had been determined to have something from the author of the thirteen-volume *Studies in the Psychology of Sex* (1897–1910). I remember the impact that work first had on me at the British Library, where I was obliged to read it in the notorious 'cupboard', away from the other library users. After donning my gloves I was soon skimming through its pages. Inversion, paedophilia, masturbation, masochism – the whole erotic life of man was present in all its astonishing variety. As I emerged I felt irremediably soiled and violated, but a strong bond of admiration had nevertheless been forged.

Dr Ellis replied promptly to my letter, saying that he would be glad to visit Westbury. He arrived at ten o'clock on an overcast September morning, and John brought him from the station in the car.

He presented a strange and compelling figure indeed as he mounted the steps to the house: a man of about sixty-five, rather bent-over, with a head of white hair which fell amply in two curtains either side of his head, and an enormous white-and-yellow beard which also stuck straight down in two forks.[2] His eyes were large and black, and seemed to stare far into space. His nostrils were as cavernous and mobile as a foal's.

We went first into the Painted Drawing Room, where Dr Ellis was much taken by the bucolic scenes of Pastorini and Barret, and examined them closely for what he termed 'overpainting'. At one point he stopped in front of a large, gilt-framed looking-glass, and seemed to examine the reflection as if it were a canvas that happened to feature the two of us: an aged sexologist and a pretty, trim young woman of just thirty-seven. We were interrupted by the maid bringing in tea and cakes, and moved away to settle ourselves on the chaise longue which had once been owned by the Earl of Rochester, and still had a stain.

Then Dr Ellis began to talk.

His first topic of conversation, which he pursued with vigour for at least half an hour, was Rembrandt's *Woman Bathing in a Stream*, the canvas in the National Gallery that shows a woman walking into a river with her legs parted and her shift held up. Dr Ellis argued that this was an 'Undinistic' study. Never having encountered the term, I asked him what it meant.

2 Someone should write a paper on the facial and head-hair of sexologists – they are a breed apart.

'It is a coining of mine,' he replied, his eyes sparkling merrily through his beard. 'It derives from the name of the Greek water sprites, the Undines. One might also use the word "urolagnia" to describe the same phenomenon.'

'Ah, you mean the derivation of sex excitement from observing the act of urination.'

'Precisely. It is my contention that this is as common a source of sexual stimulus, or in the Blochian sense, a perversion, as, for example, sexual attraction to animals.'[3]

'I don't quite see the connection with the Rembrandt picture.'

'That is hardly surprising. I believe that the woman in the picture was originally depicted as urinating, but that the falling stream was later painted out. This vandalism – there is no other word for it – was no doubt committed from misguided motives of morality, perhaps shortly after its creation, perhaps by the National Gallery itself when they acquired the picture in 1831. If the latter, then it had survived in its original state for nearly two centuries.' He gazed wide-eyed at me, and I realized that I could have been anyone – the maid, Rembrandt himself – as long as I was prepared to listen to this thesis.

---

3 Iwan Bloch, of course, held that perversions were the normal expression of erotic preferences established in childhood because of 'accidental external conditions' – such as growing up on a stud farm – or in adulthood by the desire for sex variety. Almost any area of the body, or any object, from a raven to a writing-desk, especially a miniature rubber one, could thus become the focus of 'perverse' sex feelings.

'Do you have any evidence for this?' I asked.

'None whatsoever,' he replied, with a tone of assurance usually reserved for the last link in a chain of incontrovertible proof. 'It is my belief that at this time in Holland it was common for women to urinate in public. Heavy skirts would have reduced the risk of detection, and the absence of underclothing meant that women could urinate freely at any time, which they did constantly beneath their long dresses in parks, gardens and streets.'

'I see… Dr Ellis, let me tell you why I asked you here today…'

'My mother, actually, was of Dutch extraction. I recall very well a trip to the zoo we took together when I was ten years old. At one point, in front of the rhinoceros enclosure…'

'The reason was…'

'I heard a very audible stream plashing on the paved stones. I looked around, and could only surmise that the sound originated from beneath my mother's skirts. We moved on, and she said to me, "I didn't mean you to hear that." Even at this early age I saw that this claim conflicted with the evident truth. It would have been very easy for her to find a ladies' room, or else move some distance off on a pretext, or even simply to stand on grass, where the noise would have been less distinct. As for her remark – "I didn't mean you to hear that" – it was simply one more proof. Obviously it meant just the opposite: "*I meant you to hear that.*"'

'Yes… I see…'

'Even today the proximity of rhinoceroses never fails to have a certain effect on me. But I digress. I have drawn up a petition to the Trustees of the National Gallery…' – he poked around in his clothing – '…perhaps you would care to sign it?' He produced from the inside pocket of his tweed jacket a piece of paper and handed it to me. At the top of the page was written in a quavering copperplate: 'To the Trustees: Given that many experts now agree that Rembrandt's "Woman Bathing in a Stream" is an Undinistic (or Urolagnic) Study, I earnestly entreat you to PAINT THE URINE BACK IN. Signed:' Underneath was his own signature followed by a rather long and lonely expanse of white.

How could I refuse him? I signed in the name of 'A. Wellwisher, Westbury Park, Dorking'.

'Thank you. It may interest you,' he continued, tucking the petition away, 'that in my proposed sexological community in Japan, I intend to encourage the practice of Undinism, as a matter of priority.'

'Japan? You have visited Japan?'

'Certainly.'

'I too! I spent a year there with the Royal Geographical Society. A fascinating country!'

'Every sexologist I have ever met has visited Japan,' said Dr Ellis. 'Magnus Hirschfeld. Margaret Sanger. Mrs Sanger has been on six lecture tours, and speaks tolerable Japanese, I believe. Wilhelm Reich – from Vienna – now spends a considerable portion of his time there. I have heard the Japanese government is interested in his orgone accumulator. And Françoise is very eager to visit.'

'Françoise?'

'My assistant.'

'Ah.'

'The Japanese have a unique attitude to these things. Many households worship giant phalluses, you know. I cannot say I am surprised that you have been there also.' He took up a cream horn. 'I plan to see what can be done with the idea of a new type of community, based in the Far East, basking in its tolerance and its thousands of years of understanding of the human condition, yet relying on the scientific insights that only sexology has so far brought into being. As the great Iwan Bloch himself said in *The Sexual Life of our Time*, sexology must be treated as the unifying science of mankind, subsuming all other sciences – general biology, anthropology and ethnology, philosophy and psychology, the history of literature, and the entire history of civilisation. Surely a society founded on sexological principles must therefore have the greatest chance of bringing the greatest happiness to the greatest number.'

I felt greatly astonished by this vision, and even though there was cream all over his trousers, refrained from spoiling the moment by wiping it off. 'My dear Dr Ellis,' I said, 'I am overcome. Indeed, I wonder whether you would care to write more on this – or perhaps on a related subject close to my heart? I ask because I am planning a new periodical which will deal with divers issues but will have a focus on the importance of birth control and racial hygiene. An essay by you would add immeasurably to its impact.'

'By God, I would! But Dr Haldane, say you will join us. Say you will join us in Japan!'

'I will! I will!' I cried.

Of course I had no intention of doing any such thing.

V

MY CIRCUMSTANCES IN 1925

Perhaps it is necessary here to say something about my circumstances in 1925. I was firmly settled in Surrey. I had at last realised my ambition to buy Westbury Park, the beautiful neo-Palladian house created in 1774 by William Lock, set in forty acres of woods above Dorking. My books *Wedded Love*, *Motherhood and its Enemies*, *Contraception: Its Theory, History and Practice*, *Enduring Passion*, etc., had sold in their millions. I was a nationally, even internationally famous figure. The anthropologist Malinowski informed me in 1923 that I was more famous in Swaziland than any other writer, and that the Chagga people worshipped me as a goddess.

In my personal life I had been less fortunate. Indeed, my book *Wedded Love* had been an attempt to put at the service of humanity knowledge that had been won at some cost. I refer to my marriage to the geneticist Richard Wriggle, which had been a dreadful disappointment. In 1916, at my wits' end, I initiated a nullity suit on the grounds of non-consummation.

The suit hinged on the rigidity of certain 'parts' of my husband. At one point the following question was posed to me in open court: 'With regard to your husband's parts, did they ever get rigid at all?' My answer was that they were never *effectively* rigid. One can of course be rigid without being effective.

(As an aside, physiologically the question was absurd, for if all Wriggle's 'parts', in the plural, had become rigid, his genital apparatus would have presented a strange spectacle.)

As I had foreseen, the ultimate success of the nullity suit proved crucial for the success of *Wedded Love*. It helped greatly to deflect any charges of immorality that such a pioneering publication would normally have attracted. The fact that I was not prosecuted for obscenity, that I remained untouchable, was due partly to the fact that I had never been 'touched'. What a loss to humanity if any other version of the events had been allowed to do its destructive work! Sometimes the letter of the law must be sacrificed to higher ends.

Wriggle failed me. He disapproved of my choice of newspaper, holding that only one newspaper was necessary for a household, and that he would be the one to choose it. He was futile and weak. Though occasionally rigid, he was never *effectively* rigid. He published very few academic papers after I married him. He threatened me with a vegetable-peeler. The marriage was not a marriage. In almost every sense, therefore, it was unconsummated.

VI

EUGENICS

There had, however, been another strand in my life up to 1925: rocks.

My father was the archaeologist John Mullender Haldane, and my uncle (his brother) John Regan Haldane, the physiologist. That they were both christened John argues for a certain parsimony of outlook in my paternal grandparents, I have always felt.

At the age of eight, my father managed to procure some fossil vertebrae from a school-friend, but when they were discovered in his possession he was soundly whipped. I believe he had left them on the stairs, causing the maid to fall and break her spine. But the punishment only fuelled his desire to know more. At thirteen he was found with fossils in his bed, and was again beaten, even more severely. As a result he joined the British Association for the Advancement of Science.

He later met my mother at the Association's annual ball at Claridge's, where she was presiding over the raffle stand. My father won a fossil of an archaic shrimp. Emboldened by this small piece of good fortune, he made his first stumbling advances towards her: he was instantly rejected. Marriage followed, and the shrimp was duly framed and hung over the marital bed.

I soon grew to share my father's love of archaeology, geology and related sciences. From an early age I had the opportunity to meet and converse with many eminent men. On one occasion, I remember,

Francis Galton came to supper. Galton, as readers may know, was one of the many highly gifted individuals in the genetically remarkable family of Charles Darwin. To my young eyes Galton always looked a little like a parrot: his upper lip curved down slightly in the centre like a tiny beak. Galton's best-known achievement is probably his paper showing that the ugliness of the women of Aberdeen is an evolutionary response to the high level of inherited macular degenerative disease among Aberdonian men.

I recall particularly a conversation Galton had with my father on the subject of the heritability of genius. On this occasion Galton had just finished demonstrating the new science of fingerprints with the aid of my infant sister, who had run off crying, and he was cleaning his hands with the aid of a teacloth.

'Intelligence, of course, runs in families,' he said, looking in the direction of my wailing sibling. 'The Bach family and the Bernoulli family spring to mind. J.S. Bach and his wife produced more than ninety-six musicians, male and female, many of exceptional talent. Similarly with the Bernoullis. Unfortunately both families also suffered from rare genetic defects.'

'Defects?' asked my mother.

'In the case of the Bachs,' Galton replied, handing her the teacloth, 'the family was afflicted by a condition known as "lobster claw", in which both hands are split down between the second and third fingers so as to resemble a lobster's pincers.'

I was six at the time, but had the presence of

mind to pipe up. 'Does that explain why Bach's music is full of such difficult octave-work?' I asked.

'Exactly so,' replied Galton, directing a benevolent gaze at me. 'Some of J.C.B. Bach's partitas are obviously physically impossible for anyone with normal appendages.'

'And who were the Bernoulli family?' asked my father, to my slight shame.

'The Bernoulli family of mathematicians,' said Galton, 'in three remarkable generations discovered many of the basic laws of mathematics, while confined to a small house in Geneva. Unfortunately they were all, without exception, covered with tough scaly skin which moulted every six months, and prevented them from emerging from their mathematical cloister into the light of day.'

I was fascinated. 'Could nothing be done to help them?' I asked.

'Unfortunately not,' said Galton, turning to me. 'But perhaps the science of eugenics may now point the way forward.'

'From the Greek,' I put in quickly. '*Eu*, meaning "well", and *genesis*, meaning "originating".'

'Again, your daughter is correct,' said Galton, beaming in psittacine fashion. 'Only six years old? Extraordinary. Yes, eugenics, simply put, is the science of good breeding. The situation of the Bernoullis, had they but known it, could have been remedied by a eugenic technique known as "out-breeding". Here the less desirable characteristics are purposely "bred out", while the desirable characteristics, such as mathematical genius, are retained. This process might have been accomplished in a few generations by selecting maidens with exceptionally fine and soft skins. These could then have been introduced into the house to use as breeding stock for the deformed, almost reptilian mathematicians, possibly under cover of darkness…'

'But what of the maidens themselves?' asked my mother. 'Surely they would have a right to be regarded as more than mere breeding stock?'

'Ah,' said Galton, 'there we have the basic problem. Whose interests should prevail? A few harmless and undistinguished maidens, or the race in general? I know which I would choose.'

Such conversations made a profound impact on my young mind, and when I came to choose my own academic career, I naturally settled on the sciences. I gained my BSc in geology in 1902, winning a scholarship to Munich. My doctorate was awarded for work in mincralogy, comparing the Mohs and Brinell hardness scales. My *Hardness* is still a standard textbook. When Robert Falcon Scott was found dead in the Antarctic in September 1912, some large rocks were discovered in his camp. He had, in fact, been collecting these for me, and had carried many of them all the way from the coast to the South Pole and partly back again. As history records, Scott's party perished quite near the food dump that would have saved their lives.

Science, then, was my childhood, my school days, my livelihood, my career – until my marriage. It was the failure of this marriage that turned me from an academic in the field of mineralogy into a campaigner for erotic rights.

Mineralogy and sex may seem to have little in

common. But my passion for the scientific method underlay them both. Science could deal with sex in a way that religion and morality could not. As I struggled in the nuptial wreckage, science allowed me to make a minute study of the problem from every angle. I made forays into the works of Weininger, Ellis, Hirschfeld and others. The British Library 'cupboard' became almost my second home. The result was *Wedded Love*, in which reason and passion were for the first time allied, and which heralded a new solution to sex difficulties based on the twin theories of the periodicity of female desire and the health-giving effects of the interpenetration of opposite-sex secretions. Following on from this work, and in response to the many pleas for advice I received, I turned my attention to contraception, opening the Mothers' Clinics in London, and later Leeds, Aberdeen, Belfast and Cardiff, for the purpose of giving contraceptive advice to working women. After they had proved successful, further clinics were opened in other parts of the Empire.[4] At every stage I had to battle the indifference, hostility and ignorance of doctors, not to mention the fact that contraception was considered little short of infanticide. However, I was given the strength to persevere by my knowledge that the lack of access to contraception routinely resulted in the untold misery of millions of working women, and the foisting of further generations of inferior infants on the world.

---

4 E.g. the Natal Ante-Natal Clinic in Pietermaritzburg.

VII

BOSIE

As my next target, I fixed on a contribution from Lord Alfred Douglas.

The poetry of Lord Alfred is, of course, among the great treasures of world literature. However, Lord Alfred himself was a Roman Catholic, and his faith had begun to tinge his poetry, a development I observed with some distress. Lord Alfred was in fact known to espouse all the reactionary politics of the Roman Church, holding that original sin was passed on through the medium of the sex act, that it was forbidden to eat the meat of hares, and so on. He had also recently translated *The Protocols of the Elders of Zion* into Aramaic. Needless to say he opposed birth control. As the nation's leading advocate of contraception, I was regularly anathematised by him in print as a blasphemer and the spume of Belial.

Now, I knew that spume simply meant froth or foam. Thinking this might effect an introduction, I wrote to him in Hove, where I knew he was living in rather reduced circumstances, kept alive mainly by his fierce wish for a Civil List pension. My letter ran as follows:

> Dear Lord Alfred,
>   I cannot quite see why you associate spume, meaning simply froth or foam, with Belial. As an aside, I have admired your poetry for many years, and wished to say that

despite our differences on the matter of birth regulation, believe you are our greatest living poet.

Yours sincerely,

Dr Amber Haldane

I received a reply immediately.

Dear Amber Haldane,

Thank you for your letter. By 'spume' I meant simply a sort of noxious by-product of the Devil – perhaps the froth engendered by a Satanic rage, or something similar, or any foul exudation of this sort. Spume is, as you say, froth, which is sometimes dirty or malodorous – you may have seen froth at the seaside like this – and this is the sort of thing I had in mind.

So, in brief, what I was aiming for was an evocation of something noisome, polluted, evil and foul. A little unfocussed as a metaphor, perhaps.

I do thank you for taking the trouble to write. I have been at death's door recently and, in the little time remaining to me, do tend to say as I find.

Sincerely,

Douglas

I replied at once:

Dear Lord Alfred,

I was sorry to hear that you have not been

well. I enclose a small bottle of Fellowe's Syrup of Hypophosphites to help you. It should be taken three times daily, with meals, and emphatically NOT drunk all at once.

As I wrote in my last, I believe that your lyrics will live long beyond the present century. When I read the productions of the 'moderns' such as T.S. Eliot and Ezra Pound I cannot help reflecting that the twentieth century has produced little of note since your 'In Excelsis' (though perhaps a word might be said for Walter de la Mare and John Masefield). Ezra Pound in fact wrote to me recently to request some advice on transliterating Japanese characters. (These days people seem to talk about nothing but Japan.) Quite frankly, I was revolted by his letter. It breathed utter poetic ignorance.

There is little point in our arguing about matters such as birth control. Friends must simply agree to differ on matters such as these. In any case, although I devoted the first half of my career to campaigning, I intend to devote the second half to poetry. I am starting a new magazine and I would be most honoured if you would agree to contribute a poem to the very first issue.

I hope this request does not offend, and I remain yours devotedly,

Dr Amber Haldane

His reply was as follows:

Dear Dr Haldane,

I combine in my veins the blood of the three great royal houses of Scotland, England and Ireland, and so I must ask you to remember this when judging my words and actions. As the result of more than a thousand years of selective breeding, I have inherited the instincts of the true aristocrat, which is to be fearfully rude to everyone – and yet unable to refuse even the smallest request from a petitioner.

I have said before now that you are spume. I withdraw it. Of course I will contribute a poem. Here it is.

Yours sincerely,
Douglas

Dear Lord Alfred,

Oh good. Did you mean to attach it?
Ever yours,
Amber

Dear Dr Haldane,

Silly of me. I forgot to attach it.
Here it is:

Sonnet

I walked by night in roseate realms forlorn
Where no live thing bestirred the midnight air,
And came upon a goatish man, a faun
All pale of face, with moon-flowers in his hair.
Said I to he: 'Why dost thou sigh so deep,

Avoiding ray of sun, here in this lonely place,
Why dost thou make lament, and creep
About? How wast it that thou fellst from grace?'

He gazed full in my eyes, all 'mazed to see
A human child address him in this fashion.
And said: 'My name is Shame, imprisoned here
In this dull garden for eternity
Because I gave myself to basest passion.'
And suddenly he grinned from ear to ear.

Yours, Alfred Douglas.

Dear Lord Alfred,

I was so moved to receive your enigmatic sonnet. Rest assured it will go in the very first issue of the periodical. My deepest thanks.

Your poetry has always moved me; I believe I was thinking mainly of you and perhaps the early work of Swinburne when, at the age of ten, I began to write my own poems. I remember writing a list of my favourite words: they were then, and remain now, rosemary, rosy, roseate, ripple, beryl, chalcedony, amber, sapphire, amethyst, aureate, valour, virginal, verdigris, vernal, viridian, vermilion and vervain. (To this day I do not know what 'vervain' actually means – I think it may be related to 'vervet', a small mammal). As Bernard Shaw once said to me, 'You are a true poet, that is, one who must write, regardless of what pressure is put upon you to stop.'

I know this is a dreadful imposition, since you must have people writing to you all the time with their poems. However, if you would indulge me, I would be so very honoured if you would read the enclosed. Tell me honestly what you think. The heights of your poetic genius are so far above my own poor talents that I am like a valley between tall hills; if a boulder of invective tumbles down from those heights the valley must not complain, but simply absorb the blow.

Here it is:

Vervain

Love bade me wait
In these primrose-dappled woods
For your sweet touch

Love bade me stay
And spend the livelong day
Here in the beryl shade

But then you came, with brow of chalcedony
And hair of amber
And rosy virginal lips

And vervain kiss! –
Like a small mammal
In the soft earth

Ah! Again and again,
On skin, and hair, and breast

The rippling life within

A fiery flame of amethyst
My senses bursting with delight
Responding

To life's joy within you.
Then, abruptly, you departed
Leaving me alone among the poppies

Exquisitely fulfilled
And still aflame, but without shame
And waiting for you to come back.

Yours ever,
Amber

Dear Amber (I hope I may call you Amber),

Thank you for your astonishing poem. It is not really my sort of thing, since I have always avoided *vers libre*. However, I see you worked in many of the words on your list, which is always the trick. I have my own list, many of which are the same as yours, by an odd coincidence. Have you thought of adding 'velvet' to your list? It is so like the other words you favour, and is so useful, that I feel I ought to recommend it. It is certainly one of my favourites. Some others, at random, are: pallid, wan, sad, clenched, alone, youth (concrete noun), purple, cheeks, grapes, moon, proud, honey, gall, pant, heaven, red, honey, purple, pant, die, fall, sleep, bother.

A vervain by the way is a type of African monkey.

With best wishes,
Bosie

Dear Bosie,

Thank you so much for your comments and advice. It is too late to do anything about vervain now because the MS has gone beyond proof stage and is due to be published next week as part of my collection *Love Songs for Young Lovers*. I should have told you before that I am a published poet, but I was too shy, I suppose. It is available from the Windmill Press.

You and I share more than one thing, it seems, despite our differences. I too have suffered at the hands of the ignorant and have undergone several trials – both literal and figurative. I know you have been involved in litigation as part of the aftermath of the Wilde trials and of course as a result of your counter-allegations that Edward Carson derived pleasure from asphyxiating himself with a silken cord – and in the presence of a good part of the Cabinet too. Do tell me about Wilde. What was he like?

Yours ever,
Amber

Dear Amber,

Except when he wanted something, Oscar was completely monosyllabic. You were lucky to get a grunt out of him. I gave him most of his best lines – *Lady Windermere's Fan*, for example, was more or less dictated by me. All of his remarks were thought up well in advance.

He was a virulent homosexual, of course, unlike myself – though I have never been opposed to Uranianism, regarding it as an unfortunate affliction rather than a crime. During the time we lived together I often remonstrated with him but he said he could no more help it than I could. He was not that type of older homosexual who perverts and corrupts the young – the type who truly deserve to be condemned, since they ruin a young man for life and turn him away from women for ever, launching him into a career consisting of nothing but poetry and litigation. He was older than I by some years, of course, and was very experienced with boys, while I was only just down from Oxford – but he was not the pattern of the predatory seducer. He would often tell me that what he sought was not base physical love, but what was pure and perfect, what was to be found in the sonnets of Shakespeare and Michelangelo, a deep, noble spiritual affection – and then I would find his hand working its way up my leg. And of course I would discover that he'd written the whole speech down well in advance. But he was so easy to forgive.

Let me know if you need anything else,
Yours,
Bosie

I was delighted to receive these letters, proving, as they did, that ideological battles were no bar to private friendships. I was touched that Lord Alfred would even consider communicating with someone such as myself, a well-known scientist and reformer – and with such warmth.

However, I did feel a little guilty that I had not told him that the projected title of the periodical in which his poem was to appear was *Birth Control Monthly*.

VIII

MR GANDHI

Around the time I was soliciting support from Lord Alfred, I read in the *Telegraph* that Mr Gandhi was visiting London.

Mr Gandhi's grievances against the British in India are well known. He is also famed for his numerous pronouncements dealing with more general matters in the moral and religious spheres.

According to Mr Gandhi, a perfectly virtuous man is one who can 'lie by the side even of a Venus in all her naked beauty without being physically or mentally disturbed.' For Mr Gandhi, virtue therefore consists of ignoring our God-given instincts to consummate the union of body, mind and soul that is the marital act.

Furthermore, I am reliably informed that Mr Gandhi has collected a number of young females, who, at different times, share his bed so that he can test this hypothesis. His favourite, I understand, is his grand-niece, Manu. Apparently she accompanies him everywhere, and while he tours India quelling inter-tribal passions, sleeps naked next to him every night.

Mr Gandhi refuses all attempts by Congress party officials to dissuade him from this practice, despite the possibility that it might attract scandal. His daily massage sessions are also usually performed by young girls, and he often holds interviews with visiting dignitaries or political leaders while they (the girls) slowly rub his naked, oiled body. Stanley

Baldwin was once entertained by Mr Gandhi in this fashion, and is said to have fled screaming after enduring a three-hour session of talks during which the Mahatma was continuously massaged with sweet-smelling oils. It is reportedly a very effective negotiating strategy.

It is also known that Mr Gandhi opposes birth control as likely to lead to imbecility and nervous prostration. Instead, he recommends that husband and wife simply avoid being alone together, since 'the only possible motive for privacy between husband and wife is sexual enjoyment'.

In view of the above, I felt it extremely unlikely that the Mahatma would wish to contribute to my periodical, but in the hope that his pronouncements on birth control might originate from mere ignorance, I telephoned him at the Carlton Hotel, where he was staying. After a considerable wait the great man finally came to the telephone.

At first it was difficult to make myself heard above the noise on the line. There was a confused billowing and slurping sound.

'Mr Gandhi?' I said. 'My name is Dr Amber Haldane.'

'Oh yes?' came a cracked voice. 'I have heard of you. My friends all write to you for advice.' He let out a high-pitched giggle.

'I am most gratified. I am always ready to help,' I said. 'But now I am phoning for a different reason. I am afraid I must be frank. India has, it is clear, the beginnings of a severe population problem. Indeed, I am surprised that you can retain the respect of millions of people when your attitude to contraception and birth control is so retrograde.'

'Ha ha ha ha ha ha!!'

'It is always the very lowest and worst members of the community that reproduce prolifically, and if populations are allowed to breed unchecked…'

'Ha ha ha ha ha ha ha ha!!'

'… producing thousands of warped and inferior infants…'

'Ha ha ha ha ha ha ha ha ha ha!!'

'… the result will be that you as a race will slide towards the utter deterioration of your stock.'

'Ha ha ha ha ha ha ha!! Ha ha ha ha ha ha ha!!'

'I am glad that I amuse you,' I said, rather losing patience.

'Ha ha ha ha ha ha ha ha!! My dear Dr Haldane! That is the best laugh I have had all morning. It is nine o'clock. Now, Dr Haldane, let us examine what you are saying. The problem, as you see it, is not the suffering borne by poor mothers by having too many children, the drudgery of childbearing, and so on, but the disproportionate increase of the C3 Indian population at the expense of the A1 British taxpayer. Is that not right?'

'Certainly not.'

'Ha ha ha ha ha ha ha ha!! And furthermore, when you speak of thousands of inferior infants, you are doubtless thinking of people like me?'

'I assure you I have the greatest respect for you.'

'Ha ha ha ha ha ha ha ha ha ha!!! But you have just told me that you are surprised that millions can retain any respect for me at all! Ha ha ha ha ha ha ha!!!'

'Like you, Mr Gandhi, I only wish to ensure the

unborn beauty of future generations. I have nothing but admiration for clean-limbed Indian manhood.'

'Ha ha ha ha ha ha ha ha!!!'

'I have published poems on the subject. You may have read them. They deal with the beautiful and strong bodies, and the clean and powerful minds, that are doubtless to be found among your people and caste.'

'Ha ha ha ha ha ha ha ha!!!'

'The desire of the Indian people for a better tomorrow, for social transformation, is close to my heart. I believe birth control has a part to play. "Babies in the right place" is my motto. This refers of course to spacing within families, not geographical distribution.'

'Ha ha ha ha ha ha ha ha ha ha ha ha ha!!!'

'I am telephoning to ask whether you would be interested in contributing to a periodical I am planning, the aim of which is to merge the great truths of all the major world religions and extract their essential teachings on such matters as the creation of a healthy, stable population, with all that that entails for the well-being of mothers and children.'

'Dr Haldane! Stop!! Ha ha ha ha ha ha ha!!!'

'Will you write something?'

'Ha ha ha! What is this publication to be called?'

'The projected title is *Birth Control Monthly*.'

'Ha ha ha ha ha ha ha ha ha ha ha ha ha ha ha ha ha ha ha ha ha ha ha ha ha ha ha ha ha ha ha ha ha!!!! Ha ha ha ha ha ha ha ha ha ha!!!!!'

'Can I take it that your laughter is a good omen?'

'You certainly can, Dr Haldane. Ha ha ha ha ha ha ha ha ha ha ha ha!!!! Ha ha ha ha ha ha ha ha ha ha!!! Goodbye, Dr Haldane!!!! Ha ha ha ha ha ha!!!'

And the line went dead.

The future of India looked bleak.

IX

PROFESSOR KEPPEL

On 8th November 1925, just over two months after our conversation about the periodical, a telegram arrived from Havelock Ellis.

HAVE ARRIVED AT SEKKUSU-SHIMA ISLAND STOP ACCOMPANIED BY FRANÇOISE PROFESSOR KEPPEL HIS FAMILY AND A BRILLIANTINED YOUNG MAN STOP WE EAT MAINLY CLAMS STOP TODAY I OBSERVED AN OLD MAN URINATING STOP YOUR PRESENCE HERE WOULD ADD INESTIMA-BLY TO THE CLIMATE OF FIERCE DEBATE AND BOLD EXPERIMENTATION STOP AM CABLING FROM ONOMICHI STOP LETTER FOLLOWS STOP YOURS ELLIS

I had spent my time in Japan largely in Tokio, where I had contact with people at the highest level of society, and where there was always noise, bustle and excitement. The prospect of joining a collection of frail suburbanites scratching a living on a tiny island digging up clams was not in the least appealing. In any case, I have always been allergic to clams.

Not long afterwards the letter itself arrived:

Dear Dr Haldane,

I trust you received my telegram. As you will now know, I am writing to you from the small island of Sekkusu-shima, between the main islands of Honshu and Shikoku in the Japanese 'Mediterranean', or Setonaikai Sea. We arrived about a week ago. It is a remarkably beautiful island, covered mainly with palms and cycads, which give out an agreeable oily smell; it is about two miles long and one mile wide, with the main axis orientated roughly east-west. The nearest town on the mainland is Onomichi, about twenty miles distant, or one afternoon by sailboat.

The weather at present is hot and occasionally thundery. The seasons in this part of Japan follow a sub-equatorial pattern, with hot summers and mild winters. On the hill at an elevation of about three or four hundred feet is a large compound of houses with tile or bark roofs, which has been taken over by myself, Françoise, Professor Keppel (formerly of the Berlin Sexological Institute), his wife and children, the brilliantined young man I mentioned in the telegram, and a Japanese couple from the Kansai University. Wilhelm Reich of Vienna will be joining us shortly, I hope, but he is presently in England at the Institute of Orgonomy in London. As part of our work here we have agreed to run tests on his orgone accumulator, which, as you may know, is a sort of hut made with walls of alternating organic and metallic layers. One sits inside to accumulate sexual pulsations.

There is a small indigenous community, mainly of fisherfolk, but the islands are also visited by a few local tourists at this time of

year, who come to bathe and to visit a water-
fall at the eastern tip of the island, near which
a shrine is located. Men and women tend to
bathe here in a state of nudity or wearing
brief cloth garments; children of both sexes
bathe naked up to the age of about eighteen,
at which point they are indistinguishable from
the adults. This all seems very promising.
There is little to indicate that the custom of
urinating en plein air is *not* generally observed
by the general population, but more observa-
tion is called for. Françoise sends her regards.

There is a steamship that leaves regularly
from Genoa on the fifteenth of every month.
Your expertise would be invaluable.

I look forward to hearing from you soon.

Sincerely,

Havelock Ellis

The presence of Professor Eugen Keppel was
intriguing. Keppel is of course known for his
hormonal experiments, particularly his efforts
to feminise male rats through castration, and to
masculinise female rats by grafting testicles onto
them. The apotheosis of his research came when
a masculinised female rat was induced to mount
a feminised male, an event which, when written
up for the *Jahrbuch für Sexualwissenschaft* in 1919,
brought plaudits from the sexological community
around the world. Keppel then moved on to the
next logical step: humans.

Briefly, the situation was this. As a child in Austria,
Keppel had noticed the enthusiastic copulations of

goats. After his triumph with the rats, his thoughts turned again to these animals, and at the same time he was introduced to a civil servant by the name of Steiner, who happened to confide to him that he was not able to achieve effective rigidity during sex intercourse. Keppel suggested, jocularly, that he try a regular diet of goat glands. Steiner replied that he would try anything, and that Keppel, as a medical man, should consider he had *carte blanche*. At that moment, two conditions for an historic experiment were met: a desperate patient and a doctor unlike any other in the world at that time. I say 'unlike any other' partly because of Keppel's knowledge of the new science of sex hormones, and his complete lack of scruple, but also more literally in that he was not, in fact, medically qualified. Keppel had never taken any medical examination, preferring to rely on what he called 'common sense.'

The treatment was simple: a matter of removing strips of goat testicle and grafting them into the scrotum of the patient. Yet the results were beyond all expectations. The patient regained his virility and praised Keppel's technique to the skies. Soon Keppel had many other patients, and began to charge high fees.

Some three months after the first operations, however, an unfortunate side effect emerged. The experimental subjects began to give off an unpleasant aroma of billy goat, which became intolerable to anyone or anything within a wide radius (except, that is, a female goat). Keppel responded in a manner which showed great coolness and presence of mind. He simply enlarged the experiment. At first he had used testicular grafts from the Angora goat, but now, in search of a solution, he explored grafts from the Nubian, Alpine, Saanen, Toggenburg, La Mancha and Oberhasli breeds. It was only when he reached the Cameroon Pygmy goat, which is only found in West Africa, that the unfortunate side effect was eliminated. By now his fees had been raised still further to take account of the live export of these exotic beasts, but there was still no shortage of paying customers.

I began to wonder whether the native fauna of Sekkusu-shima included any goats.

Keppel was rich and successful, but his critics were multiplying. This was partly because the efficacy of the goat-gland transplants tended to tail off in the long run, requiring more and more frequent operations, but also because he had branched out into other areas of sex science. His attempts to cure homosexuality, for example, by introducing the gonads of a heterosexual criminal into a passive, homosexual young man, resulted merely in a homosexual criminal who refused to pay any fees and stole ten thousand marks in cash, as well as some jewellery, from Keppel's wife.

Keppel's mistake stemmed from his faulty understanding of the way glandular extracts worked on his experimental subjects. Opposite-sex secretions, he considered, cancelled out or transposed the sex characteristics of the subjects. Yet, as my own observations proved, opposite-sex secretions rather accentuated and fostered the characteristics of the male or female concerned. Moreover, Keppel's fixation on invasive procedures such as surgery and injection was unnecessary, for glandular extracts could be taken orally with much less discomfort. It was superfluous to ask a doctor to inject his patient three times a day, when the patient herself, without too severe a strain on the memory, could take three gelatine sperm-pills in the morning, afternoon and evening.

In 1924, Keppel finally overreached himself by using an aeroplane to dust a district of Munich with three tonnes of crushed puppy testes in order to observe the effect on birth statistics. Retribution was swift. He was investigated, his lack of academic qualifications was uncovered by a newspaper reporter, and he was forced to retire from practice. No one knew where he had gone.

Until now.

X

THE MEETING WITH H.G. AND BOSIE

There were many decisions still to be taken regarding the future of the periodical. With these in mind I arranged to meet Bosie and H.G. for tea at the Ritz.

I have always enjoyed the Palm Court. The pastries are excellent, and the pianist, Humphrey, has a very nicely shaped head. Of course, the Ritz is difficult to book at short notice, but it so happened that the day-manager had once written to me for advice on premature ejaculation, and a quick telephone call to refresh his memory of this fact was enough to secure us a table. Bosie expressed some alarm on hearing that I had invited H.G., but agreed to meet us nonetheless, asking only if he might borrow the train fare from Hove.

It was around a quarter to twelve when H.G. and Bosie arrived at the Palm Court. They came in together, and I supposed they had met in the lobby. Bosie was dressed in a baggy suit of late Victorian vintage, the trousers of which hung listlessly in swathes from his fifth waistcoat button, not quite reaching his shoes. He gave no sign of having been the 23-year-old exquisite who had so captivated Wilde. His once flaxen locks were grey, though still curled wildly around a now balding pate; his once marmoreal features had metamorphosed into those of an ancient Queensbury, with down-curving mouth, contemptuous half-unaware eye, and nose of huge and bulbous cast, with a tip of dead white.

H.G., on the other hand, was well turned-out, in a smart light-coloured suit with a narrow striped tie, though it did not conceal his gain in weight. He was as near globular as any science-fantasy novelist I have ever met. Both men seemed to be puffing slightly, and Bosie's nose was in an early phase of excitement, the upper part flushed with a dull red.

'My dear Amber,' H.G. said eagerly as he sat down. 'I have discovered I can stop time. By a sort of mental flexion, I can command everything to simply… halt in its tracks.'

'Nonsense,' said Bosie flatly.

'Then how do you explain the following?' asked H.G. 'This morning, a little over half an hour ago, I was walking through Russell Square. Suddenly I realised that of all the many scores of passers-by, I was the only one moving. Even the motor cars and 'buses had stopped. The people were suddenly as fleshy dummies, unbreathing, suspended between moment and moment. I looked around in amazement, then approached one, a young woman. Fearing for my sanity, I reached out a trembling hand. As soon as I touched her breast, it was as if some command had been given. The spell shattered; she recoiled and screamed something, and then the square seemed to come to life again.'

'Armistice Day,' I said after a moment, putting an éclair on a plate and passing it to him. 'You yourself are wearing a poppy.'

H.G. took a bite of the éclair and reached for the teapot, his eyes all the while fixed on mine, the look of eagerness on his face strangely undiminished.

'Now, my friends,' I said, 'our publishing

undertaking is on course for a tremendous success. I have the feeling that this will be a historic encounter, and when I have this feeling I am usually right. One of the first tasks that we, the editors, must undertake is to choose a title for the periodical. I suggest something descriptive such as *Birth Control Monthly*.'

Humphrey launched into a rendition of 'My Chilli Bom Bom'.

'Am I to understand this periodical will give succour to the godless doctrine of birth regulation?' enquired Bosie. 'If so, I will refuse to have anything to do with it. Oscar did not believe in birth regulation, and neither do I.'

'Not at all,' I replied soothingly. 'Its aim will simply be to discuss, in a free and fair way, this and other important issues of the day, giving both sides. That is why you, as our greatest poet, will have such an important symbolic impact.'

'Why not then *The Contraceptive Agnostic*,' put in H.G. 'Since you have not made your mind up.'

I shot him a quick glance.

'Not a bad idea,' said Bosie, 'but since Mr Wells is planning to contribute, perhaps the title should appeal more to a mass readership. How about something such as *Time Travel Weekly*.'

'Or perhaps *The Independent Catholic Digest*,' H.G. said.

'Or *The Giant Ant Digest*.'

'Or *Papal Tips*.'

'Or *The Linen-Drapers' Gazette*.'

'Now, now,' I said. 'There is no need for bickering, though perhaps it is inevitable that our two greatest literary talents should find themselves in some measure in disagreement. But let us pool our differences. Of course you both know that I have devoted my life to the cause of the working woman, to the improvement of her lot and to the expunging of the vast mass of worthless and idle individuals brought into being by her feckless and uncontrolled breeding. It is no secret, even from you, my dear friend' (here I looked at Bosie, who managed a sour twitch of the lip), 'that I have ever opposed the doctrines of the Catholic Church, and have, as a result, found myself the victim of a campaign of persecution that has not been seen, perhaps, since the days of Cardinal Bellarmine.'

'Mind if I light up?' H.G. asked.

'But I am not principally concerned,' I continued, ignoring him, 'with those obscurantists within the great mother Church who seek to retard the development of humanity. I appeal instead to those who can look forward to the future. It is in the name of the fine, clean-limbed men and women of the future that I asked you both to meet me here today. We three are visionaries. We are advocates for the good.'

'Of course we are, otherwise we wouldn't be here,' said Bosie, gesturing around him at the Palm Court, Humphrey and the assembled tea-drinkers. 'But we must also know what we oppose.'

'Certainly. We set ourselves firmly against those who would demean all that is pure and noble in men and women. In every human there is a spark of the divine. To foster it we must eliminate all that is base and servile, all that is mean and ugly and bestial.' I turned to Bosie. 'Will not you, as a true Catholic, and as the greatest writer of sonnets in

English today, lend your weight to my crusade for the betterment of mankind?'

'My dear Amber. Why is it so difficult to refuse you? I shall want paying.'

'Of course.'

'What about the title?' asked H.G.

'Perhaps on reflection we should leave that for later,' I replied. 'No doubt something will emerge.'

'Very well.'

'Now, as I see it,' I said, 'the periodical will include not only campaigning articles but also general developments in sexology, and poetry.'

'What do you suggest I focus on in my first piece?' asked H.G.

'Well, you could turn something out on the theme I was developing just a moment ago. The future of humanity. Eugenics.'

'Ah, yes, a fascinating area.'

'The science of good breeding,' remarked Bosie rather pointedly.

'Eugenics,' ruminated H.G. 'You mean something on the future evolution of our species. A future in which our unborn offspring will be half human and half machine. Or perhaps we will split into two races.'

'Why not three?' said Bosie.

'Three, then. Of course, there is the interplanetary aspect to consider. A eugenically engineered race – or races – would need to evolve to exist on other worlds, in which the atmosphere, gravity and so on would be completely different.'

'Keep your feet on the ground, man,' snorted Bosie. 'Sinful man is restricted to Earth. There is no superlunary Wild West. Sin, atonement, redemption, that is the true cosmic drama, played out in the here and now, and in the hearts of men. I have never believed in space travel. It is an essentially Protestant idea.'

'There is no reason to suppose we will not take our churches and our totems with us into Outer Space,' H.G. said. 'That too is part of what it means to be human.'

'Ridiculous,' spat Bosie, his nose livid. 'You realise you are talking to a scholar of Aramaic. I ought to strike you down.'

'Quite,' said H.G., not appearing to hear this remark. 'Quite. Excuse me for a moment.'

He got up from the table and ambled off.

'I am astonished that anyone wants to read his books,' muttered Bosie. 'He is clearly insane.'

'H.G. is eccentric, certainly, but he has been invaluable to the cause of birth control.'

'No doubt he sees it as a pretext to meet lady reformers and bluestockings. Women always seem ready to swallow a good deal of him.'

H.G. returned quickly to the table. 'I thought at first that it was some sort of wraith,' he said, 'but it turns out to be the actual incarnation of my editor, Adolf Papp. Now I am afraid I must leave.'

'So soon?' I asked.

'I am afraid so. I must talk to Adolf urgently about my next, *102 Ways to Write Stimulating Books*. The deadline expired this morning, and he is most anxious that I finish writing it – beyond the title, that is. He is waiting for me outside. I will look forward with the keenest interest to any news on *Birth*

Control Monthly. Forgive me, please. I bid you, dear Amber, and you, my dear Lord Alfred, good day.'

'Good day,' said Bosie with finality.

The sage of Bromley departed the Palm Court.

XI

A CONVERSATION WITH MR MASEFIELD

H.G. and Bosie were valuable gains indeed, and would ensure a wide readership. Nevertheless, other, younger men must also be enlisted if *Birth Control Monthly* were truly to represent the voice of the young century. Names came readily to mind. John Masefield, Walter de la Mare, Siegfried Sassoon, Edmund Blunden – the virtues these men embodied were re-emerging with new strength and beauty after the shattering convulsion of war.

The poetic arts had always been an important facet of my own career, of course. I well remember a conversation with one Dr Blinkenhorn, an old professor of Literature, who told me that in due course I would forget 'all this scientific nonsense' (I was studying in Munich for my doctorate at the time) and realise that my true métier lay with the plangencies of the written word. I must have protested. In fact, I remember protesting quite forcefully. We were waiting for a tram outside the university, which always makes me cross. I attacked him with some ferocity, I remember. At the close of my harangue, he merely laughed – a little brokenly, perhaps – and repeated, 'You will come round to it in time – you will recall our conversation.' And he was right. He had fathomed the unexpressed idealism at the centre of my thoughts. By the end of that decade, although immersed in the scientific work that was to bring me to prominence, I had produced my first collection, *To Love*, which, in a sequence of sonnets[5], traced the moods wrought in the mind of a growing girl by the study of geology, with an emphasis on morphology. It was followed by *Keroro*, a long poem presented in semi-dramatic form, with parts played by a 'He' and a 'She' who have met and repeatedly loved in aeons past, interwoven with all that matters fundamentally in mineralogy, through the characters of the Spirits of Earth, Rocks, Air, Trees and other Elementals. I quote briefly:

> HE: My sweet! This rose,
> Whose petals my lips press
> Is kept in all its beauty cool
> By myriad xylons
> That cunningly doth it refresh
> With sweet liquids.

> SHE: All beauty's functions spring from desire.
> As in bituminous coal, whose fire
> Derives from the compacted plant remains
> Of myriad lovely roses.

If it were truly to advance the cause of reproductive reform, *Birth Control Monthly*, I decided, must publish that poetry which bore the mark of the deep experience of the human heart – the heart that exults, above all, to love.

Of course, there were other currents in the literature of 1925 that were not so salutary. The

---

5 The sequence used is an invention of mine, later dubbed by George Bernard Shaw the 'Haldaneian stanza', with varying lengths of 13, 14 and 15 lines.

proponents of 'modern' obfuscation were abroad. To them, poets such as Masefield and Blunden were out of date. Obscurity, arcane reference, muddled thinking, rejection of rhyme, abandonment of rhythm, evacuation of sense – these were the new standards. It was not uncommon, in the little magazines, to come across verse such as the specimen below:[6]

b-w-l-r-o-i-c-t-k-e-r-s
I
s(it)hero(nthe)
GR(BLOCK)ASS
Iserablym
F(OO)
  St
    r!
        ugg
  ling4
    rutter
ants
    '*(** ▽° **)*'
O(le)n(adi)l(ngto)y(more)
BlOcKwRiTiNg

Birth Control Monthly would set its face against this obscurantism.

Of the poets mentioned five paragraphs ago, among the most familiar names to many readers will doubtless be that of John Masefield, the 'Poet of the Sea'. I, like many others, had often thrilled to his hearts-cry for tall ships, his tales of adventure on

---

6 By an American, admittedly.

the swelling main, his portraits of obdurate villagers and shiftless town-dwellers – so much so, that when he wrote to me with a sex problem, I decided that a visit would not go amiss. His problem in itself held few features of real interest, but it would give me the opportunity to discuss the contribution to *Birth Control Monthly* that I hoped to extract from him. I felt strongly that the first issue would not be complete without a contribution from his pen.

He was, as it happens, living at that time in the lighthouse on St Anthony's Rocks off the coast of Weymouth: an attempt, as he later told me, to 'get as close to the sea as possible without actually being in it'. I arrived in the early afternoon of Friday 17th November 1925, in calm weather and a golden late-autumnal mist, by hired sea-aeroplane.

Doubtless having heard the noise of the 'plane, they were both waiting on the jetty: Masefield himself, a mustachio'd, balding, slightly bent and flinching man in early middle age, wearing dark spectacles, as if he had recently been exposed to some strong light; and his wife, Constance, an attractive woman with a rather absent air, who looked as if she had done nothing but eat and read for the last six months.

'I am so pleased to see you, Mr Masefield,' I said, stepping ashore. 'I usually charge two guineas an hour, but in your case I will waive the fee. First, if I may, I would like to speak to Mrs Masefield alone, then perhaps you and I can discuss a subject dear to both our hearts: Poetry.'

'Very well,' Masefield replied in sombre tones. 'I will wait in the watch room.' He entered the little door of the lighthouse, with Mrs Masefield and I following behind. We soon settled ourselves in the 'water parlour' on the lowest floor, where there was a crackling fire, gaily-coloured knitted rugs, book-shelves and a small galley kitchen.

'Now, my dear,' I began, 'your husband's letter states that he is presently inhibited from sex activity.'

'Oh yes,' Mrs Masefield replied casually, turning down the hood of her sou'wester, and revealing as she did so a spill of flaxen hair. 'That is so.' She reached behind the settee to put a kettle on the hob. The water parlour was rather cramped. 'Of course, we would never have spoken of this to anyone other than you, Dr Haldane.'

'Naturally. So, please tell me – what do you feel is the trouble between you?'

'John has certain ideas about physical relations,' she continued. 'Possibly they have evolved during his close reading of the works of Tolstoy... I fear also that he has become gradually enervated by the labour involved in our life here.'

'Is there a great deal of labour?'

'The lighthouse is mechanised, naturally, but he insists on propelling the beam around by hand.' She turned a pair of storm-blue eyes to the ceiling. 'He says it is his penance – for what I'm sure I don't know – but since he can only push at a fraction of the speed of the motor, the result has been that a number of ships have foundered in recent weeks. This has tended to add to his self-torment.'

'I see.' I frowned.

'Is there any cure?'

'Let me speak to him.'

Mrs Masefield called her husband down from the watch room, and I now had a better chance to look at him. He was still mustachio'd, balding, slightly bent and flinching – though perhaps more so than I had at first noticed. The knees on his trousers were almost entirely worn through, perhaps from prayer, perhaps from crawling on hands and knees, or else a combination of both.

I reflected that I should try to steer a course between the helpful, on the one hand, and the draconian, on the other.

'Mr Masefield, I would first like to say how much I have enjoyed your work.'

'Thank you.'

'I particularly enjoyed your *Salt-Water Ballads*.'

'Very kind.'

'I have spoken to your wife, and would like to ask you a few simple questions.'

'All right.'

'To what do you attribute your current inhibition from sex activity?'

Masefield glanced hesitatingly at Mrs Masefield.

'I was raised in the country,' he began. 'You have read my poems of country lads and maidens, honest and plain-speaking?'

'Certainly.'

'I knew before I was six years old the facts of life – who would not? I knew too what went on in ricks and barns and fields once the pubs had shut up for the night. I knew every Jack had his Jill.'

'Yes.'

'Jack, drunken and lustful. Jill, wanton and eager.'

'Yes.'

'And I saw what happened to the babes they couldn't keep. Helpless souls that came in glory and went out in fire.'

'Yes.'

'All wrong! Men behaving like the beasts. Only worse than beasts, because we knew better.'

Mrs Mansfield brushed a stray curl from around her neck.

'I see,' I said. 'May I summarise? Your current reluctance to engage in coitus is a result of feelings of disgust, primarily of religious origin, for what you see as an essentially degrading and animalistic activity.'

'Maybe the beasts are better. For a man, it is... it is like playing in a stinking ditch...'

'Yes...'

'...like being covered from head to foot in the most revolting stuff, and never being able to wash it off.'

'Mm...'

'And yet...'

'And yet?'

'And yet at the same time I am drawn to it by a force stronger than I can withstand. My God!' he ejaculated. 'Stronger than everything I hold dear! I feel constantly drawn' (here he inhaled tremulously through his nose) 'to degrade myself and my poor wife with the most vile and loathsome practices imaginable!'

His wife, lighting a cigarette with her right hand, reached for Masefield's knee with her left, and patted it.

I held up one finger. 'You have been conditioned,

I perceive, at an early age, to despise a fundamental, God-given aspect of our humanity. You require a complete re-education. Now, please take this down verbatim.' I held up another finger, then let both fall, then held the first up again. 'Firstly, love between men and women should never be left simply to unregulated desire. That way lies the guilt and shame that you have been describing. Regard your connections as an act of sacred love and duty to be observed almost as the Christian rites you were schooled in. Thereby your unions will be sanctified as if by the power of the universe itself.'

'Yes…'

'The burning magnificence of an overpowering lifelong love, completely free of guilt and shame, is available to all. The secret, based on extensive research into the mystic tides of the female sex-rhythm, is for the male to restrain himself for periods of a fortnight, after which there may be union. Then allow another fortnightly period to elapse, according to this graph.' I produced a copy of my graph 'The Periodicity of Recurrence of Natural Desire in Healthy Women', and handed it to him. 'Now, it is important that you observe the following rules. Firstly, never attempt connections during the proscribed period. A strong will can calm the nerves which regulate the blood supply, and command the distended veins of the male organ to retract.'

'I see.'

'However, be aware that when the tides are up, you must approach her immediately. Not to do so will bring disaster.'

'Tides. Yes…'

'In the intervening periods do not fall prey to incontinence. As Sir Thomas Clouston writes in his book, *Self-Pollination*, death can easily result from such practices.'

'Yes.'

'Do not achieve the climax of your own pleasure too quickly; however, do not draw out the experience for longer than her nerves can stand; do not practice *coitus interruptus*; and do not be either prudish or careless.'

'Careless…'

'You must woo your wife before every act of coitus. Not to do so would make you guilty of rape. Make absolutely sure that your wife experiences pleasure during these connections. Not to do so will cause her numerous nervous and other diseases. She will moreover be deprived of healthy sleep.'

'Yes…'

'Do not yourself fall asleep immediately after intercourse. You must be prepared for extensive post-coital discussion as an essential adjunct to the act itself. Women use these moments to unburden themselves of the many small confidences, doubts and accusations they have been storing up over the previous days and weeks. Now remember – here I come to your general attitude towards your wife – she is not a man and does not think as men think. She must feel that she is the centre of your thoughts, wishes, hopes and desires. Do not cause suffering to your wife either by comparing her directly or indirectly to other women, or, alternatively, by placing her on a pedestal apart from the rest of womankind.'

'No.'

'As man and woman, your twin roles in the drama of marriage are distinct. Man is still essentially a hunter. It is he who experiences the thrills of the chase, he who continually dreams of ascending Mount Cithaeron and surprising Diana unawares at her bath. Do you have a bath?'

'Yes.'

'Good,' I said. 'Put your wife in it.'

'Wife… in bath.'

'Yes.' I paused. 'To recapitulate: restrain yourself, then approach her at exactly the right moment; beware temptation in the intervening period; have a regard to her female pleasure; regulate the blood supply; do not achieve your own climax too quickly or too slowly; avoid *coitus interruptus*; do not be prudish or careless; woo your wife before coitus; ensure she achieves healthful sleep; respect her feminine sensibilities, which are more delicate than you can imagine; yet hunt her down and attack her like a wild animal when she gives you the right encouragement. Do not misinterpret her almost imperceptible signals, or you risk utter catastrophe. All this will, I am sure, be more than enough diversion from the remnants of faulty upbringing that disturb you.'

'I beg your pardon,' interjected Constance Masefield, causing me to start. I had forgotten she was there.

'Yes, my dear?'

'Is there some way in which I could help?'

'There is no question of that, believe me. Such a thing is completely unnecessary.'

'Oh good.' She paused. 'Do you know – I think I have forgotten to fill the hot water bottles. It is wise to warm the beds early at this time of year. Do please excuse me.'

'Certainly, my dear.'

John Masefield watched as Mrs Masefield ran lightly up the stairs.

XII

A CONTRIBUTION FROM DR ELLIS

I left Masefield with a copy of my poem, 'Flux'[7], and received his assurances that he would forward something for the magazine as soon as possible.

Shortly after my return I received another letter from Havelock Ellis:

> Dear Dr Haldane,
>
> I am most pleased with the development of our new community.
>
> Professor Keppel has set up a laboratory in which he is performing some experiments on the local fauna. There are no large mammals to speak of, much to his disappointment, but there are ducks, and it is towards these that his researches have been directed. His theory, I believe, is that since some ducks are naturally hermaphroditic, duck glands can be used to induce spontaneous hermaphroditism in humans. A close watch has been mounted on the kitchens.
>
> My assistant Françoise has added a great deal to the life of the community. Her original name, Cyon, she has changed to Delisle, which is an anagram of 'de Ellis'. Since we

---

7 Printed privately. It deals with the establishment and maintenance of a healthy erogamic relationship in words comprehensible to denizens of London's East End, and has been much distributed as a broadsheet at the Mothers' Clinics and door-to-door.

first met a few years ago she has proved most receptive to my ideas. One one occasion she agreed to put my urolagnic theories into practice in the middle of Oxford Circus; I was so delighted I could have kissed her. Frau Keppel disapproves, but it is difficult for her to climb upon any moral pedestal because of the activities of her husband. Of course we keep her too under constant surveillance.

The brilliantined young man remains something of an enigma. No one knows who he is, why he is here or how he came to accompany us on the steamship from the mainland. He rarely speaks, and spends much of the time alone. When he does appear he is always dressed with faultless taste. He is a person of great beauty. His moustache, black, is superbly curled at the tips. Whatever anyone says to him he receives with an expression of grave consideration. He plays the flute very well, and often favours us with a haunting rendition of 'Sakura', the notes of which can be heard to throb the length and breadth of the island.

We usually dine *al fresco* on a long table overlooking the ocean. Many of us dress in kimono, which I have introduced as preferable for freedom of movement. Our diet has improved. We now have soft-shell crab, tinned peas, tinned tomatoes, tinned soup and strawberry jam.

Every afternoon Françoise and I bathe. We often encounter fishermen, and the fishing here is done in a way I have never before seen. The fisherman stands in the stern of the boat holding six or seven cormorants on long leashes. The cormorants, which are purposely starved, dive into the water and catch fish, before returning to the boat, as they think, to consume them. They are however unable to swallow the fish because of the tightness of the cords around their throats, and a little further pressure on their throats from the fisherman is enough to encourage them to disgorge their catch. We were all fascinated by the process, particularly Professor Keppel, who was afterwards seen enjoying a lengthy conversation in broken Japanese with one of the fishermen.

I spend much of the time writing, and have already produced several essays and poems. I enclose one of the former for the periodical we spoke of.

My valedictions from our little paradise,

Yours truly,

Havelock Ellis

The essay began as follows:

A Nipponese meditation

It so happens that my life has brought me to a little island in a little sea, and here I am content to spend my days under the shade of the palms, caressed by warm breezes, looking out to the west as the great turquoise rollers advance and crash on the strand.

The majestic flying of spume is constantly present. Here nature carries on with her work as she did before that troublesome creature, man, arrived, with his grasping appendages, his hungry mind, his yet-hungrier mouth, and his tinned food.

One morning on the beach I espied a young native girl, standing just where land takes over from shore, amid the grasses and bamboo groves, a girl in a shift of printed yellow cotton. Her black hair hung down her back in a rich and wild cascade, casting upon her shoulders strange and ever-changing shadows. She had the face of a courtesan in a Hokusai woodblock, brown eyes under black brows, a jewel-like mouth, smooth round shoulders, and below them, firm, statuesque and shapely breasts, marvellously virginal, the very embossments of femininity. Behind, her counterposing globes gave no sign of the slight dejection that often accompanies later life and the cares and wearinesses of maternity. She walked, she strolled, she sauntered on the sward, her body in motion a multifarious dance summoned from the recesses of ancestral race-memory, the neatly fitted joints, as they moved, effecting the most minute attrition, abrasion or limature on one another, massaging and caressing themselves, tinily auto-osculating until any watcher might loudly and involuntarily groan, his being a welter of turbulent amazement. Such experiences remind us that our response to the physical beauty of persons is an eternal duality, that is, the aesthetic, on the one hand, and the animal, on the other. If we allow the animal to dominate, if we are ravished beyond reason, then we fail to penetrate beyond, and into that quality which, as Kant terms it, is the *ding-an-sich*, ontological reality, or, in the deepest interpretation, the divine. But, on the other side, if we allow our appreciation of beauty only to operate on the aesthetic plane, then we deny the insistent stream of longing for union, for completion, that lives within us. The aesthetic and the animal are therefore themselves like two rivulets. As they course through us, each intertwines with, interpenetrates and subtly refreshes the other. I remember an experience I had in a urinal in Montevideo which brought this home to me with unforgettable clarity, though this is perhaps not the moment to go into it.

We ignore the things of the body at our peril. We are, after all, the products of evolution. The spasmodic flailing limbs of the chimpanzee as he leaps with antic un-gainliness around his cage in the zoological gardens, give rise, through the alchemical transmutations of natural selection, to the liquid grace of a Pavlova. Even the rhinoc-eros has much to teach us. The shameless outpouring of dung and urine that we witness when we stand in front of his enclosure is the self-same end-product of our own processes of ingestion and digestion, processes that lie

at the root of our humanity; and all our arts
and sciences are no more than raucous howls
of delight and defiance as we void ourselves
into the forests of primaeval Night. Civilised
man recognises this by cloaking these processes in a ritual so holy that it can only be
performed in private, enclosed and solitary, a
jealous guard placed on the greatest mystery
and the greatest beauty of all...

There was much more in the same vein. As I read, I
recollected strongly the emotions I had experienced
so long ago in the 'cupboard' in the British Library,
where I had first encountered Ellis's *Psychology of
Sex*. Several of the ideas the little essay touched
upon were close to my own concerns, particularly
the emphasis on the fundamental pulse of the
body, which relates naturally to the occurrence of
the female sex-rhythms that I had recently spent a
pleasant afternoon discussing with Mr Masefield
and his wife.

And indeed, what could be simpler than for a
man to restrain himself for periods of a fortnight,
in order to conform to the rhythms of his mate?
This, after exhaustive experiment – on myself and
others – was at the core of my new solution of sex
difficulties. I proposed that there was in woman's
physiological life a definite sex-rhythm with two
crests or peaks, one just before the onset of men-
struation, and one approximately half-way between
one menstrual period and the next.

In some women the wave-crests might be somewhat depressed due to fatigue and over-work. In

this case the best remedy would generally be a bracing iron tonic, or complete rest and possibly a visit to some vitalising, sunshiny region, such as the Swiss Alps in winter, where the entire system could be returned to equilibrium. The women of the East End were often greatly astonished to learn that the Swiss Alps were only about as far from London as London is from Edinburgh, and were accessible almost as cheaply by rail.

The dual wave-crest theory had two important corollaries.

The first was that woman's sex energy was entirely independent. Woman was not a dormant object to be awakened by the touch of a man. Her sex energy was an inevitable rising and falling, as unstoppable as the sea, the motions of the planets, or the seismic shudder of the earth's crust. Her tides came to full flood twice a month, and would do so regardless of the presence of a person of the male sex.[8]

The second corollary was, surprisingly, that men's sex energies could easily be made to conform to the same fortnightly pattern. A fortnight was, in fact, the perfect period in which men could restrain themselves to advantage – neither too long nor too short. During the period of adjustment to the new

---

8 One society woman, a conscientious and devoted wife and mother, confided to me that at these times in her regular cycle, she would feel so aroused that she would sometimes rush out of the house, emitting shrill keening cries, and prey on the gardeners. When her husband returned he would often find her semi-conscious and covered in soil. She was, she confessed, not 'in her right mind' at these times.

regime, of course, the man might experience some difficulty weaning himself away from the selfish and instantaneous satisfaction he had previously regarded as his birthright, and he might feel, as a result, the build-up of an almost intolerable head of pressure. But this reserved sex energy could be diverted into all sorts of useful work: the instruction of the young, hammering, ministering to parishioners, and so on.

During this period of restraint on the part of the husband, the slow electrical surges of his wife would themselves inevitably be gaining in frequency, beginning, to be sure, from the complete and total ebb-tide of passion (when she might feel all but uncomprehending of the purpose, nature and even the existence of sex-feeling), but growing stronger as the days and weeks passed, until deep-hidden memories of sex-desire began to awaken, hormones began to course joyously into her bloodstream, sex-feeling began to dominate her workaday concerns and finally to drive out any other coherent thought.

Meanwhile her husband, brought to the brink of insanity by his own dammed-up glandular secretions, would have become nothing less than a slavering animal.

It is at this point that the fortnightly congress occurs.

It is wild, feral, ungovernable. No quarter is given or expected. Congress is repeated, again and again and again, in a racial frenzy that neither of them until now had imagined possible.

At last the repeated unions become more and

more leisurely, and the stage is gradually reached in which both husband and wife are left spent and exhausted, drowsing languidly in one another's arms in the immemorial embrace that enables each to absorb fully the vital health-giving secretions, through their respective epithelia, of the other.

The next morning the husband is heard whistling cheerfully at his shaving-mirror. He is again healthy and relaxed. He is able to address himself wholeheartedly to all manner of good works. No longer preoccupied and bedevilled night and day by excessive desire for sex intercourse, he has a sense of vitality and self-command. Indeed, he may well wonder what madness possessed him in recent hours to assault his beloved wife in such a fury of rapine. The wife, for her part, though perhaps a little chastened and astonished by his rough embraces, is secure in the love of her husband, and bathed in the nutritive fluids he has supplied. Her whole system is brisk, healthy and toned.

It is in this manner that a healthy and harmonious marriage, enriched by enduring love and respect, can be achieved until the very end of life itself.

These ideas were, I felt, at the base of Dr Ellis's interesting contribution.

XIII

DR REICH AND DR HARVARD

'My colleague, Dr Harvard,' said Dr Reich.

Dr Harvard bowed. He was a thickset young man, with closely cropped hair that stood up in bristles. He was wearing a white laboratory coat.

'Dr Harvard is head of our bio-electrical department,' said Dr Reich. 'We believe that the rise and fall of electrical potential over the skin surface can be measured to determine the orgastic potency of the subject. We take a control area of the skin's surface such as the leg, and compare its potential to areas of the body that are most sensitive to sexual stimulation, such as the penis, vaginal mucosa, anal mucosa, tongue, nipples, and in some subjects who have more than the average mental endowment, the forehead.'

I nodded, looking around me. The occasion was my first visit to the London Institute of Orgonomy, founded and led by the famous Dr Wilhelm Reich of Austria, author of *The Function of the Orgasm*. Dr Ellis's recommendation of Dr Reich had convinced me that the new currents in sexological thought might be worth investigation, possibly with a view to soliciting a contribution to *Birth Control Monthly*. I had also read that Dr Reich was something of a literary man, several of his works, such as *Genitality in the Theory and Therapy of Neuroses*, being couched as fictions. Accordingly, I had decided to visit him in Walthamstow, a sleepy suburb to the north-east of the capital.

Dr Harvard nodded, breathing loudly through his mouth. 'Ja. Ve measure ze skin potential in five different situations. Ze single subject engaged in self-stimulation. Ze single subject who is orally-inclined being administered sugar or salt. Ze couple engaging in kissing and touching. And ze tickling of ze subject viss a feather or cotton wool. It is important not to tickle directly as finger contact might distort ze surface potential.'

'That is only four,' I said.

'I counted ze kissing and touching as two.'

'Ah yes.'

'In ze kissing and touching experiment viss ze couple, each of ze subjects is vired up so zat opposite electrodes are placed into separate bowls of electrolyte solution, viss ze man sticking his finger in one bowl and ze voman in ze other. Ven ze couple engages in any sexual contact, such as some forehead-to-tongue stimulation, ze circuit is completed and ze result recorded on an oscillograph. It is unfortunately not always possible to continue measurements up to and including orgasm because ze violent movement of ze subjects tends to dislodge ze electrodes.' Dr Harvard thrashed his arms about wildly and laughed.

'Do I detect a Bavarian accent, doctor?' I asked. 'Forgive my curiosity, but I have never heard the name Harvard, apart of course, from the American university. Is it German?'

'I found zat my original name voss unpronounceable when I vorked in ze United States, so I changed it to Harvard, because I voss living at ze time near ze University of Harvard.'

'Oh, I know Professor Walker at Harvard, in the Biology department. And Professor Bennett, of course, the geologist.'

'Ah ja. Unfortunately I did not have ze opportunity to visit Harvard itself, but I stayed very close, very close – undertaking my own research.'

'Dr Harvard had to leave the US recently after falling foul of a quite ridiculous statute against moving animal semen over state lines,' said Dr Reich. 'So we count ourselves very fortunate to have acquired him here at the Institute.'

Dr Harvard bowed again. 'It voss very unfortunate but it voss a matter of some importance in my research and I voss unfortunately not in full compliance viss ze local laws relating to ze movement of semen for artificial insemination for farm animals. Of course, I voss not in possession of semen from farm animals.'

The two doctors laughed heartily.

'No, I voss possessing mainly mouse semen, viss also some bat semen and a liddle canary semen. I voss at ze time undertaking experiments on semen, to prove zat ze ejaculate of a bat contains ze air pockets zat make it lighter for flying. For me zis voss my research, nothing more. Semen of all kinds is my meat and drink, you know.'

'I understand.'

'Well,' said Dr Reich. 'Thank you, Dr Harvard. I can see you are keen to get back to work, so we will leave you alone.'

'It has been my pleasure.'

Dr Reich ushered me from the room and out into the hall. The Institute for Orgonomy was in fact a small terraced house, rather cramped, cold and dank. Where we now stood in the hall, the floorboards were bare, and large patches of rot had destroyed much of the plaster.

'Now, where next,' mused Dr Reich.

I confess I had not expected to find him quite so charming. I knew, of course, the basic facts. He was a Marxist and an atheist. He had been a student of Sigmund Freud at the Institute for Psychoanalysis in Vienna, and so had been trained under the aegis of that dubious science which has done so little to foster a healthy attitude toward sex relations. Freud, after all, linked the origin of neurotic symptoms to sex episodes in childhood, which, as anyone could see, was putting the cart before the horse.

Reich had – to his credit – made the break with Freud, and had achieved a therapeutic reputation of his own, though not without controversy. He was still young, not much older than thirty-five, a bear of a man, with a manner that alternated between geniality and menace. His most noticeable feature was a shock of blond hair, so light as to be almost white, which stood straight up from his head and waved gently as he moved, like a stand of bleached grass. I had frankly never seen anything like it, and wondered whether there might be some bio-electrical cause. His speech, despite his middle-European origin, was distinctly American in tone.

'You must excuse the appearance of the Institute,' said Dr Reich equably. 'We are not quite ready to open fully yet but we hope to do so in a matter of a few weeks. I have just returned from Illinois, where the first college of Orgonomy is based.'

'There was one thing that puzzled me a moment ago, Dr Reich,' I said. 'What did you mean by the term "orgastic potency"? This is what your electrical experiments are designed to measure, if I understand them correctly. Yet I confess that in the course of my own scientific training I have never encountered it.'

'It is my own term. It is a measure of the ability for total surrender to the involuntary contractions of the organism and the complete discharge of excitation at the acme of the genital embrace.'

'How does it differ from a normal orgasm?'

Dr Reich turned and looked directly into my eyes. We stood closely together in the rather confined space where the hallway led to the rear of the property. 'The difference,' he said in a low voice, 'is fundamental. You may rest assured of that, my dear Doctor.'

'I should like to know more.'

He raised his chin, still meeting my gaze. 'Have you ever thought what it would be like to divest yourself, if only for a moment, of all psychological and physiological constraint? To forget false morality and society's strictures? To conquer the plague?'

'The plague?'

'The emotional plague that afflicts all mankind. The plague that limits true orgastic potency. Most of our administrators and politicians suffer from it. That is why politicians walk the way they do. Have you ever noticed how cabinet ministers walk?'

'Well, I have always propounded the idea that natural orgasm is of inestimable value. A large part of my work has been to do with freeing normal sex life from the shadows of repression and nasty-mindedness.'

'Good for you,' said Dr Reich, with a sudden jolly grin. 'Then we are confederates, you and I. We certainly subscribe to nothing nasty or unwholesome here at the Institute.' He peered through a small glass panel in a door that led off from the hallway; on the door was tacked a sheet of paper bearing the words 'Character-Analytic Vegetotherapy Department'. 'Ah,' he said. 'Now, unless I miss my guess, a therapy session with Dr Aslan is in progress. Yes, an interesting case. A mother of five children, all in good, responsible jobs, all crippled by mental illness, and blaming her.'

'What exactly is vegetotherapy?'

'The term derives from the vegetative or autonomic nervous system. It has nothing to do with vegetables.' He laughed pleasantly. 'People often think it does, and so think it is something crazy. No, it centres on the idea that normal and healthy childhood emotions such as fear or anger are suppressed as the child grows to adulthood, and that these emotions become trapped in the body.'

'Ah yes.'

'We have found that the human body has seven segments held in place by a muscular armour. Emotions become trapped in the armour and must be released.'

'I see.'

'False moralities. The prohibitions of prophets, Jesuses, Buddhas. This is the worm in man. We try to break down the armour and release the flow of energy with a regime that involves kicking, rolling the eyes, biting on soft objects and screaming.'

I looked through the small window in the door. Dr Aslan, I saw, was a woman, about fifty-five years old, of Middle-Eastern appearance, full-breasted, with a graying bun of hair. Her laboratory coat was open, with underneath a red organza dress and a necklace of greenish glass beads. The patient was also a woman, also in middle age, wearing only her underclothing, stretched face down on a single bed, her hands near her mass of brownish hair. Her face seemed to be resting on a medium-sized toy rabbit made of cloth. Over her prone body Dr Aslan slowly moved a device, consisting of a small, battered wooden box, painted sky blue, with seven or eight metal tubes protruding from it and a larger rubber tube running away and disappearing under the bed. As we watched, Dr Aslan made an indistinct command. The woman suddenly emitted a muffled whimper, easily audible through the door, and began pounding her fists into the pillow either side of her head, kicking her legs and bucking her body; at the same time she reared her head up so that I saw for the first time a purple, swollen face, with mascara-covered eyelashes and heavy bags under the eyes. The stuffed rabbit, I now saw, she held in her jaws; it quivered violently. Both doctor and patient seemed to catch sight of us at the same moment, and, as if in response, Dr Aslan quickly whipped the rabbit from the woman's mouth. 'What do you want to do?' Dr Aslan demanded in a resounding voice. The woman, baring her teeth, let out a series of loud, staccato belches, looking directly at us through the glass.

'Excellent,' said Dr Reich, moving away. 'Memories associated with certain emotions are stored, in this patient's case, in the back. The muscles are chronically contracted, but the energy is freed as it is allowed to move up the body, through segments that have been freed in previous sessions, and out through the oesophagus. We always work toward the head. I hope the therapy did not disturb you.'

'Please do not concern yourself,' I said. 'I have seen destitute half-maddened creatures in the slums of the East End behave far worse than that. I only wonder about the general efficacy of such treatment.'

'Believe me,' said Dr Reich, jabbing a thumb in the direction of the room, 'That dame is approaching a complete cure. She was on the verge of developing cancer. Now thanks to the skill of Dr Aslan and the DOR-buster, she is likely to make a full recovery.'

'Doorbuster?'

'D-O-R. Deadly Orgone Radiation. The DOR-buster was the device you saw Dr Aslan using.'

'Dr Reich, I find your methods intriguing. Perhaps now is the time to tell you why I asked to see you today. I am currently planning a periodical, the aim of which is to combat false and damaging dogmas and to enshrine a normal, natural and healthy attitude to sex life. I wonder if you would be interested in publishing a paper on some aspect of your work here at the Institute. You will have complete freedom in your choice of subject – although, of course, you must bear in mind that it is intended mainly for married people. Feel free to attack organised religion. I have come to you because I have heard many people speak highly of you – Havelock Ellis for example.'

'Havelock is a great friend. I aim to visit him in Japan shortly. He's got some kind of community there. What do *you* think of Havelock? Is he in his right mind, do you think?'

XIV

AN EARTHQUAKE

Two days later I received a telephone call from H.G.

'Have you heard about Havelock?' he asked.

'Anything in particular?'

'His sexological community has been destroyed in an earthquake.'

'In what sense?' I asked carefully.

'In the sense that it is in *The Times* this morning.'

'But you never read *The Times*.'

'I happened to see it in the public library.'

I rang off immediately and picked up my own copy. After some searching I found an article on page 32:

SEX COMMUNITY DESTROYED IN EARTHQUAKE

By our Tokio correspondent

Sekkusu-shima Island, central Japan. The earthquake of 19 November, which measured at nine on the Mercalli Scale, destroyed a controversial settlement founded by writer and scientist Dr Henry Havelock Ellis, it emerged today. The community was set up earlier this year with the intention, in the words of its founder, of 'freeing man's sexual life from centuries of superstition', but now lies in smouldering ruin. At least three people died and another two were injured on the island when the earthquake struck at four o'clock in the morning.

Mr Ellis, interviewed on Tuesday, commented that the quake 'was a tremendous rocking and shaking, like being swept down a surging river on a high-frothing wave'. He and his co-worker Françoise Delisle managed to escape outside during the earthquake, as did Mrs Elizabet Keppel, another resident of the community, and her son, Helmuth.

Dr Ellis continued: 'After only a few short moments of calm, the shaking recommenced, with even greater violence, and in front of our horrified gaze the four main buildings collapsed. We ran around the perimeter of the buildings, calling out to those still within. We soon heard sounds from within the third house. It was the brilliantined young man, who was buried under some large object.'

Dr Ellis was unable to give any further details on the identity of the young man. 'It was still dark but we were able to see, through a crack in the roof, moonlight reflecting off his head,' he noted.

Those who died in the incident were later revealed to have been Professor Eugen Keppel, formerly of the Berlin Sexological Institute, who was wanted for questioning by the Munich police department regarding a series of dog thefts, the Keppels' daughter Eva, and Kengo Matsushita, Assistant Professor of Sexology at Kansai University. Mrs Assistant Professor Tanaka, who had been knocked unconscious, was eventually found alive with a dislocated shoulder.

> Frau Keppel and her son are expected to
> leave the island later this week.

This, I supposed, was the end of the sexological community. I wondered what had happened to the brilliantined young man, since he appeared to have survived. I then cabled a friend, Professor Fujii of the Kyoto Botanical Gardens, requesting that he send food parcels. Then I myself made up a parcel which I sent from Dorking. It included coffee, cheese, smoked sausage, smoked turkey, candles, crackers, chocolate, boiled sweets, powdered soup, a copy of my collection *To Love*, canned fish, mixed fruit sponge pudding, Valentine's Meat Juice, and brilliantine.

XV

SOME THOUGHTS ON ORGASM

Still greatly saddened by the earthquake, I concen-
trated on my plans for *Birth Control Monthly* and on
my work at the Mothers' Clinics. It had been difficult for some time to find good nurses, and I was
forced to set my own examination in order to screen
applicants. It was a half-hour paper with a choice
of three questions:

1) If you were asked to give advice on achiev-
ing conception to an obese woman with a
hare lip who wished to marry a negro, would
you do so?

2) Why do you consider Dr Haldane's methods to be correct?

3) In your view, is it appropriate in a Mothers'
Clinic to have photographs of babies on the
wall? Why? (Note that this constitutes *two*
questions: you should give equal time to each.)

I also contacted Dr Reich by telephone to tell him
about the earthquake, assuming that he would
abandon his plan to visit Japan. I did not find
him at home, but the telephone was answered by
Dr Harvard, who informed me that Dr Reich had
heard about the earthquake and had brought his
travel plans forward.

'But surely Dr Ellis will leave the island now?'

'No,' said Dr Harvard with Teutonic finality. 'Dr Reich received a telegram from Dr Ellis yesterday, after your visit, announcing his intention of staying on ze island. I believe zey are rebuilding ze houses. Dr Reich thinks it is vital at zis time zat zey receive supplies and equipment, and of course his special support, to help zem recover from zis tragedy. He is sending another orgone accumulator since I believe ze first was damaged in ze earthquake. You cannot have too many accumulators, you know. It vill accompany him from Genova. Ze full-size.'

'The full-size.'

'Ja, plus ze orgone boxes for re-charging food and ze orgone pads for application to ze head, orgone mattresses, *und so wiete*, or for general use.'

'I am sure that will be a great help,' I said, putting the telephone down.

Orgone accumulation had been something of a mystery before my visit to the Institute. I was now better informed. Orgone energy was not simply bio-electrical sex energy, nor merely equivalent to the vital force: it was the very essence of the physical universe. We were continually bathed, it seemed, in orgone radiation. When the body had soaked up enough of this energy, it discharged it in the form of an orgasm. However, orgastic potency could be limited by the body's inability, because of muscular armour, to gather environmental orgone. The solution was the orgone accumulator.

This was a large box-like device, made with walls of alternating organic and metallic layers, that one could sit inside to recharge oneself. I had seen one at the Institute; it resembled an upright sarcophagus. There was a small pane in the door, and inside a seat and some books. On the door was a notice, which read:

> **Caution!** Over-use of this accumulator could lead to orgone overdose! If this occurs, please leave the vicinity of the accumulator and apply to the Doctor immediately for treatment!

Dr Reich's emphasis on the importance of orgasm was, with some qualifications, sound, although his therapeutic approach was of course fundamentally misleading, damaging and wrong.

Since the publication of *Wedded Love*, and the decade of free discussion that it had inaugurated, I had often had occasion to meditate on the place of orgasm in sex contentment. Perhaps central to the cause of all sex pathologies was the failure to see the act of union as essentially a subtle balance of attributes and conditions in which there was a 'triple consummation', or perfect fulfillment of spiritual, physical, and reproductive criteria.[9] This triple consummation required of the human duity performing the marital rite an almost mathematical or syllogistic concentration at every stage. Failure to conform to any of its strictures would inevitably

---

9 The latter might seem a surprising thing for someone such as myself, who is largely associated with family limitation, to insist upon, but I am not of course opposed to the multiplication of the human race – as long as it involves the production of healthy, clean-limbed offspring, who will benefit society, and not a horde of diseased wastrels.

lead to sex pathology in which physical orgasm – or lack of it – could come to dominate at the expense of other components.

In the course of my career I have received thousands of letters from men and women expressing anxiety in this area. The following comments are representative:

> 'I have read your books with great attention particularly with regard to female pleasure and the structure you call the *glans clitoridis*, which I attempted to find. My wife however will have none of it nor the kissing of the breasts that you mentioned nor any other "wooing" before intercourse, she just wants to have it and be done with it and won't have herself messed about with, as she calls it.'
>
> Mr E.

> 'I have purchased *Dr Foote's Plain Home Talk, and Social and Sexual Encyclopedia*, and wrote to you because I found in it nothing about the female orgasm you mention. However on the way to the postbox I was struck by lightning, and the letter was burnt up.'
>
> Mrs A.D. Fey

> 'The reading of your books while sitting down made me feel so sexual that any adjustment of my sitting position made me come off.'
>
> Master B.

'My husband never stops. He says he will get what he wants regardless and he pursues me all over the house until he gets his "rights". My son meanwhile who lives with us is a victim of shellshock and while my husband and I are tearing up and down the stairs he is shouting and smashing up the furniture.'

Mrs Daniel Hole

'I write on behalf of a friend whose husband doesn't always take care to see that she experiences pleasure in sex intercourse and as a result suffers from sleeplessness, melancholia, bad temper, hysteria, jaundice and neurasthenia. So 'on edge' is she at being left without physical satisfaction by a husband whose only care is for his own needs, that she is prey to all manner of morbid and resentful thoughts – and is at the same time stimulated to sex fantasy by almost anything: novels, horseback riding, perfumes, corsets, feather beds, prolonged mental effort, pockets, bananas, society, solitude, rocking chairs, oil paintings, etc.'

Anon

'I refer to your book *Enduring Passion*, where you write, "The intense pleasure gained from clitoral stimulation is no excuse for neglecting the internal cervical orgasm. Clitoral stimulation, if practiced too frequently, or alone in the absence of cervical stimulation, or clitoral stimulation followed by insufficient time in the vagina, is likely to leave a woman exhausted and should be avoided." Well, I have tried to maintain a balance between internal and external stimulation and I find myself hopelessly muddled up. My wife is no help, as she says my referring to your books while engaged in sex consummation puts her off.'

Mr F. Clamme

'I am a normal man of thirty-six, a doctor with a medium-sized practice and wife. It took me two or three years to persuade my wife to undertake anything. When she does submit to my embraces it is often with extreme reluctance ... I decided to explore the problem scientifically, to get to grips with it in a campaign of psychological and physiological investigation, to study and explore her needs with as much sensitivity and delicacy as I could muster. For this purpose I set up a controlled experiment. I hired a young girl as a maid who was exactly like my wife in outward appearance, and, using the maid as my control, set up a battery of tests.'

Dr Vinzenz Bot

'By dint of learning Sanskrit I have managed to peruse some ancient texts which have enabled me to prolong a single act of coitus, through the use of boron suppositories, to an "all-night job" lasting eight hours, forty-five minutes and sixteen seconds. I trust this is of use to you in your researches.'

Major Q.

It remained to be seen, from Dr Reich's contribution to *Birth Control Monthly*, whether or not he would be able to tear himself away from the notion of the orgasm as the sole desideratum of a fulfilling sex life, and integrate it into a more complex model of human sex needs.

XVI

THE KING'S HALL MEETING

The first issue of *Birth Control Monthly* was rapidly taking shape, and I felt that some sort of public meeting for its promotion would not go amiss.

Public meetings are important for three reasons: they mobilize public support; they raise funds; and they allow ordinary people, mothers, etc. the opportunity to come into contact with the educated and intellectual classes.

My speakers would need to be chosen carefully. H.G., undoubtedly, would speak. H.G. is popular with ordinary people, though he needs supervision. Another possibility might, I thought, be the contralto Dame Clara Butt, known for her remarkable range and her patent laryngeal tonic, 'Butt's Elixir'. Dame Clara had been a supporter of birth control from the earliest days, and could often be seen at society functions with a contraceptive sponge attached by a scarlet ribbon to her waist. On one occasion she had gaily auctioned herself to the highest bidder to support a boys' club, safe in the knowledge that the sponge would ensure that no possible adverse consequence could arise from such behaviour. A third speaker might be Sir Aylmer Maude, the translator of Tolstoy and former Groom of the Stole (former, that is, because he had been caught trying, at my instigation, to introduce the 'Pro-Race' into the most carefully guarded boudoir in the land, and ejected in disgrace). Of course I made it clear that each of their speeches should be limited to ten minutes or less. I myself would give the keynote speech, lasting not more than an hour, with the working title 'Should we Spread the Streets of our Cities with Ever-Thickening Layers of Human Protoplasm?'

H.G., Dame Clara and Sir Aylmer all accepted my invitations; and, as the date, I fixed on the 28th of November, at the King's Hall, Aldgate. It was advertised a week beforehand using sandwich-men. Sandwich-men are the best advertising method, since they are cheap and highly visible, and cannot defend themselves. One may put anything one likes on their boards. For example, I was recently able, at the very reasonable cost of 20 shillings, to employ five men to walk up and down Regent Street for eight hours bearing boards that read simply: 'The Mensinga Cap Lacerates the Female Organ' ('Vagina' would have been two shillings cheaper, but would not long have survived the attentions of the constabulary). Bills were also distributed, bearing the words:

BIRTH CONTROL MONTHLY
NEW PERIODICAL

A
Lecture by
AMBER HALDANE,
Author of *Wedded Love*, *Flux*, etc.
With introductory speaker Mr H.G. Wells,
Author of *Mr Pippin's Trip to Alpha Centauri*, etc.
And other guests
28 November 1925
King's Hall, 6.30pm

... with a design showing a black lantern upon which the words 'A Light in our Racial Darkness' were picked out in white.

When the day came, the hall was packed full and the air warm and with an agreeable smell of iodoform, possibly emanating from the many mid-wives present. H.G., as planned, rose first to speak amid the potted palms. I could give his speech here, or a précis of it, but I am afraid I found it rather unhelpful.

Dame Clara Butt then delivered a reminiscence of her childhood in Sussex, which rambled seemi-gly to no purpose, while the audience grew restive, some sections of it apparently expecting her to sing. Dame Clara is of course best known as the pop-ularizer of Sullivan's 'The Lost Chord', and I am afraid a chant of 'Lost Chord! Lost Chord!' started to develop. Just as Dame Clara seemed to be on the point of yielding to her admirers, I saw by my stop-watch that her ten minutes were up, and escorted her from the podium.

Sir Aylmer then took the floor, and gave an account of a scene he had personally witnessed at Tolstoy's estate at Yasnaya Polyana. A young disci-ple had one day run up to Tolstoy and crashed down at his feet, confessing that he had eaten a vegetable. Tolstoy, astonished, told him that, as a vegetarian, eating vegetables was perfectly permissible, and that only meat was forbidden. The young man, horrified, replied: 'Meat! But I have been living on steak for the last three months!' The audience laughed heartily at the joke (as I presume it was), but I could see no relation to birth control, until

Sir Aylmer went on to give the reason for Tolstoy's vegetarianism, which was to combat sex feeling: the Master regarded this as 'a fundamental evil', and sex expression in general as 'wallowing in the slime of moral degradation'. At that point I noticed that Sir Aylmer's eight minutes were up, and so took the podium myself. I was wearing my white décolleté dress and hat with the lily-of-the-valley and have rarely felt more confident.

I waited until the audience had entirely settled, then spoke in a soft voice calculated to carry to the very back of the auditorium.

'God's supposed revelation to mankind two millennia ago,' I began, 'was made in the unhelpful atmosphere of paganism in the Roman Empire, in which slavery was an everyday outrage, women were treated no better than chattels, and snakes, bulls and giant insects were worshipped, as in the novels of our friend Mr H.G. Wells.'

A small cheer.

'But today I say to you that there has been a new revelation fitted for the 20th century, in which science has shown us the true path. That new revelation is the gospel of birth control.'

'Hallelujah!' someone shouted. There was some laughter.

'Now, no animal is willingly celibate. All animals, including human beings, desire union, in which they merge the wave-crests of their bliss in the ocean of cosmic space, and the heat of their contact vaporizes their mutual consciousness in burning flux.'

Yet more laughter, this time for unknown reasons.

'However,' I continued, 'the result of this sex

activity, if left unregulated, is nothing short of calamity. The very classes who contribute least to society spawn with untrammeled energy. I invite you to imagine a pyramid.'

'All right, dear.'

'At the top are professional people, and at the next level, the managerial classes, followed by the service industries, then foremen, general workers, miners, and finally, at the base of the pyramid, unskilled labourers. Now, as we descend, we see a queer thing taking place. We see that the birth-rate per couple increases steadily, while the general intelligence level proportionately decreases. At the very bottom of the pyramid – those levels buried beneath the sands of the Egyptian desert, if you will – are hopeless mental defectives, whose talent for reproduction is quite fearsome. This is a problem for which our present leaders and politicians seem to have no answer. But of course there is an answer. Birth control. The birth of children, accomplished down the ages through chance and in ignorance, must henceforward be accomplished through love and in knowledge.'

A smattering of applause; but before I could resume, another interruption from the floor.

'Yes, but what?'

A general hubbub.

The speaker stood up. He was a shabby man clutching an umbrella to his breast.

'I hope you will forgive me, Miss Haldane,' he said. 'I have been an admirer of yours since *Wedded Love* days. But we really must know which methods of control you recommend. It is most confusing.'

He sat back down as if jerked by a string, but another popped up not far away. This time it was a woman in a hat with cherries.

'It's the cats,' she said.

'Cats?' I asked.

'I tell 'em, the girls, to put the balls away, but the cats get hold of 'em.'

Light dawned. 'I see,' I said. 'You refer to balls of rubber, sometimes encountered as a contraceptive measure. I do not encourage them. As you say, they look like ordinary playing balls. If they are used in games of rounders or rackets there is a danger of bacterial infection at a later date. And of course cats must never be allowed near any contraceptive device. Cats do not deserve their reputation as clean animals.'

'What about the joey?' asked a rough male voice from the back of the hall.

'Joey?' I asked.

'He means the johnny,' said another voice.

'The joey!' came the rough voice again. My questioner, quite possibly a fruiterer, was unwilling to surrender the word.

'The male sheath, or condom, has been employed for centuries, of course,' I said. 'There is evidence that they were in use at the time of the Great Fire of London. Several lightly-charred examples were found among the papers of Pepys, for example. However, the use of the sheath prevents the absorption of the nutritive substances present in the semen…'

'Semen!' came a shout. It is a common experience, when speaking in public, that one member of the audience persistently echoes the last word one has said. Possibly it is a form of derangement.

'… and vaginal fluids.'

Before I could continue, a wet cough announced yet another interlocutor. This time, by his garb, he was a man of the cloth. He had a small beard, eyeglasses, and a rather dissatisfied look. For some reason, vicars follow me around wherever I go and they are rarely less than troublesome.

'Personally I have always practised,' the man said, 'the form of truncated union known as *onanismus conjugalis* , "masculine prudence", "self-control", or, in the more delicate vocabulary of our continental neighbours, "La Chamade" – "the Retreat" – or "*La Belle Discrétion*"…'

There were murmurs of dissent, perhaps incomprehension.

'… but I must say,' – he paused to cough – 'that it seems to me to be a rather unsatisfactory method. The effect, if I may say, is that just at the point where the male desires complete freedom of all his, ah, emotions and reflex actions, and just when the power of conscious control of the nervous system is rapidly draining away from him, as he, ah, ah, precipitously approaches the zenith of maximum excitation, then…' He gulped.

'Get on with it!' came a cry.

'At this moment,' the clergyman continued, 'he is required to exercise the most careful watchfulness and complete regulation of all his activity in the physical arena, with regard to the, ah, female partner involved. The strain is so great as to destroy, over the years, his general health, rendering him thoroughly nervous and run-down, and, in fact, inducing specific symptoms of neurasthenia bordering on insanity.'

The Reverend broke off to indulge himself in a coughing fit that seemed to go on a long time. Finally he sat.

'Well, I said, 'I fear you have given a sufficient demonstration of the consequences of withdrawal, as it is perhaps better termed. I cannot recommend it. I have further found it particularly inappropriate for men of the cloth. The consciousness of re-enacting the Biblical sin of Onan means that some clergymen are in nightly fear of being slain by a vengeful Deity.'

'Well, what, then?' asked not a few voices.

'I am happy to recommend...' I began.

'Gold spring!' shouted one voice.

'I cannot recommend the gold spring,' I said. 'It drops out of the cervix.'

'How about the Dutch cap?' screeched a bedraggled female.

'If you mean the Mensinga cap,' I said, 'I regard it as harmful.'

There was an outcry. 'What's wrong with it?'

'Its tendency is to expand the vaginal canal unwholesomely, which is injurious for most British women, though Dutch women and Americans are evidently built rather differently. For certain abnormal or fat women, however, the Mensinga cap may be useful.'

'Bosh!' cried a woman fitting those descriptions. The cry was taken up in other sections of the auditorium.

'A more serious objection, perhaps,' I shouted – I was now forced to shout – 'is the metal spring in the rim. It is liable to burst open and lacerate the male organ or surfaces of the vagina during the final and most active moments of coitus…'

'Ohhh!'

'… or during orgasm. I therefore, on all these counts, condemn it…'

'What's orgasm?'

'… except for very fat women with short forefingers or very fat women whose internal organs are already grossly stretched and displaced.'

Shouts.

'If you will give me leave… if you will give me leave… As a result of my years of experience at the Clinics… the principal method I recommend is the high-domed rubber cap which I have patented as the "Pro-Race"'.

'Pro-Race!' screamed the echoer.

'After insertion into the vagina, it is pressed around the cervical neck, where mild natural suction holds it in place. Stupid and nervous women sometimes require more detailed instruction on the correct method of insertion, but its use is self-evident to women of normal development.'

'Am I normal, dear?'

'For storage when not in use, the "Pro-Race" should generally be kept underwater…'

'Suction!' cried the echoer, rather late.

'… in a small china or celluloid pot or jar at a temperature of about 19 degrees Celsius, or *slightly below room temperature*,' I cried.

'Who do you think you are telling poor women

what to do?' Cheers and whistles.

'The "Pro-Race" comes in several sizes suitable for English women. With extra sizes for the deformed.'

Tumult.

'I'll give you extra sizes!'

'It's the cats!'

'Suction!'

'The joey!'

The first three rows of the audience, as a mass, rose to their feet. Evidently someone had recruited a mob from among the parasitic and degenerate parts of Aldgate and Whitechapel, and given them instructions to disrupt the meeting. Amid the barracking, shouting and milling, there was a general surge towards the stage. Just when the rebels had gained the steps to left and right, and disaster seemed imminent, Dame Clara, who alone remained immovable beside me – H.G. and Sir Aylmer having fled to the wings – rose from her seat by the *Washingtonia* palm, fixed the rioters with a magnificent glare and opened her mouth.

> *Seated one day at the organ,*
> *I was weary and ill at ease,*
> *And my fingers wandered idly*
> *Over the noisy keys.*

Her voice was a rippling, translucent cascade. The militants halted in their charge.

> *I know not what I was playing,*
> *Or what I was dreaming then;*

But I struck one chord of music,
Like the sound of a great Amen.

A great sigh broke from a hundred throats. Dame Clara, voice flooding the auditorium, now moved to take centre stage; I relaxed my grip on the lectern.

It quieted pain and sorrow,
Like love overcoming strife;
It seemed the harmonious echo
From our discordant life.

An enormous narcotic had descended on the heads of those present. Delicately, I took a few backward steps, and, encountering no opposition, moved into the wings. The audience continued entirely rapt, like animals stunned for dispatch.

I have sought, but I seek it vainly,
That one lost chord divine,
Which came from the soul of the organ,
And entered into mine.

In the wings I found H.G., puffing on a cigar.

'Congratulations,' he said. 'They were with you right up to the last moment, when you called them "deformed".'

XVII

A CONTRIBUTION FROM MARGARET

Just as I was composing an account for Margaret of the success of the King's Hall meeting, a letter arrived from Margaret herself.

> Lovely one,
>
> I am sorry to have been so long in writing, but my time has been taken up in all sorts of trials, libel suits, campaigning for Revolutionary Socialism, promoting the Mensinga cap, fielding the demand for my books, and hurling incendiaries in the teeth of law, custom and ignorant prejudice.
>
> I imagine you've heard about dear Havelock. I had only just returned from Japan when the earthquake struck, and intend to go back as soon as is feasible. There are good boats leaving from Genoa, though the staterooms are damnably small.
>
> Please find enclosed a contribution for your magazine. It is the only kind of writing I know how to do, which is to write *the whole thing at once*. While editor of the *Woman Rebel* I also found that it was a good idea to get banned from the mails, since the publicity value is incalculable. Try to think of something shocking to say!
>
> With all best love,
> Margaret

A small part of the contribution was as follows:

WHY DO I REVOLT?
by 'HUMBLE PIE'

BECAUSE I have seen the bodies of brave women left broken in the streets in the wake of unarmed protest, previously having been drained and exhausted by endless labor, bad food and inadequate housing;

BECAUSE I oppose all Rockefellers and Croesuses who break strikes using the paid myrmidons of the 'law';

BECAUSE I refuse to serve exploiters who desire only human flesh for their factories, for their houses of prostitution, and for their wars;

BECAUSE I am disgusted by the incense-heavy hypocrisies of the Roman Catholic Church, Baptist Church, Methodist Church, and all bloodsucking priests, inquisitors and their supporters;

BECAUSE I hate the dead hand of Charity;

BECAUSE I have had my fill of the hyenas of respectability;

BECAUSE I am full of flame and honey;

BECAUSE the best fun I have is stirring up ignorant oxen who are the slaves of convention and 'good deportment';

BECAUSE this is the hot stuff;

BECAUSE I do not buy the legal defense bunko;

BECAUSE marriage as we conceive it is

continuous sexual slavery and enforced motherhood;

BECAUSE woman is treated as a mere incubator, a breeding machine;

BECAUSE I am more than just the motive power of a mangle;

BECAUSE I am the mistress of my own body;

BECAUSE I believe in precautions against impregnation;

BECAUSE it is not murder or a crime against God, though it may be a crime against the State or Mammon, to remain unmarried and unparturient;

BECAUSE I do not wish to become the brood-mother of a warren of filthy, half-witted, feeble children, sapped eugenically until they approach the reasoning power of fish, to cook and clean for them endlessly, and to drag myself back to my endless toil after every new and exhausting birth;

BECAUSE I do not wish that my own children burden the world with another generation of human lampreys, which will then go on, unceasingly spawning, to reproduce human misery of its own, *ad infinitum*;

BECAUSE Mammon's twin loves are births and funerals;

BECAUSE I demand the right to indolence;

BECAUSE I wish to create;

BECAUSE I wish to destroy;

BECAUSE I wish to sow discord;

BECAUSE I wish to sow harmony;

BECAUSE I desire freedom;
BECAUSE I demand the right to organise;
BECAUSE I am patriotic (it pays);
BECAUSE I am meek and mild;
BECAUSE, America, I am putting my shoulder to the wheel;
BECAUSE I have brain and brawn to do so,
and am not particularly busy over the next six
months;
THEN let me rise up and smash every institution that oppresses women, after which time,
if the evils I have described have not passed
away, then let them all utterly bury me.

POEM
by ANNA PAEST

What is this whisper that I hear, softly in the streets at dawn and
at dusk, but growing ever louder, ever clearer?
Pause a moment from your toil, factory-hand, shirt-waist stitcher,
nurse, milker, sexual slave, wife – can you hear it?
Louder and louder it comes, with unrest and feverishness (like a
sick woman who has endured countless pregnancies and knows this
to be her last, and for what?)
Hungry and poor, driven to extremity by judges, landlords, rulers,
hangmen, procurers, abortion-doctors, regular doctors, cannibals,
industrialists, Friends of the Working Man, religious reformers
and wild-eyed zealots, specialists, Humanitarians –
Do you hear it?
It is the human gunpowder of your liberation and mine, the
marching feet of the striving masses.

THIS JUST IN:

Rockport, New Jersey. A jobbing journalist, learning of his wife's confinement and delivery of triplets, and unable to provide for them, hanged himself today. His existing family of fourteen was already ragged, undernourished and feeble-minded with it. The note he left said simply: 'It was my pleasure to breed uncontrollably; now it is my pleasure to die.'

LETTERS TO THE EDITOR

Madam,

Hurrah for the _____ (insert name)! It is about time we had a paper that said it like it is! This is the real hot stuff! There is nothing I enjoy more than reading about spirited women who are not afraid of anything and have that 'go-to-hell' look in their eyes!

I have been a bachelor for many years and I know it is very reprehensible even to associate with free women who don't give a damn. But I am tired of seeing girls and mothers drained and exhausted by endless labor, bad food and inadequate housing, and exploited by bosses and lackeys. There's no spunk left in them at all.

There are legislators in this city _____ (insert name?) that I know for a fact use preventives and then pass edicts stopping contraception legislation, and who use prostitutes and then make speeches fulminating against street-women.

I am just a member of a local council and a schoolteacher but if your program goes ahead it will be the greatest revolution since beef was corned and I for one will take up the cudgels and support it to the hilt. Keep up the hail of lead!

Yours etc.

Madam,

Great God! What a sheet! The other day I was perusing a copy of your _____ (insert name) on the El and a man came up to me and said to me outright that even if I had the face of an angel, I must have the heart of a devil if I read that stuff. I told him that the true devils were leering hyenas and the exploiters of women, and that the _____ (insert name) was on the contrary the spirit of freedom, the voice of the unconquerable masses, a sublime and unapologetic dedication to the female principle in the cosmos. We got friendly after that and he has become quite converted to the cause of the _____ (insert name)!

Yours etc.

CHRISTIANITY VS THE FEMALE
   by 'HUMANA'

Tertullian was not among history's better-known woman-lovers. 'You [Eve] are the devil's gateway… You destroyed so easily God's image, man. On account of your desert, that is death, even the Son of God had to die.' Eve stole an apple worth a few cents and could not afford legal counsel. Because of her trifling mistake over a piece of fruit, all women from now until Judgement Day are to be punished. Well, we salute that venerable greybeard of the Church, Tertullian. How right he has turned out.

Clement of Alexandria is recorded as having said that all women should blush, simply because of their nature as woman. Augustine, in the fourth century, in between visiting brothels, believed that although men were created in the image of God, women were created in the image of something else, which he left unspecified. 'Make me good, but not yet.' And 'Saint' Thomas Aquinas in the thirteenth doubted whether women were human.

These developments in Christian theology were not accidental. The New Testament is a primer of anti-female execration.

Colossians 3:18: 'Wives, submit yourselves unto your own husbands, as it is fit in the Lord.'

I Timothy 2:11: 'Let the woman learn in silence with all subjection.'

I Timothy 5:14: 'I will therefore that the younger women marry, bear children, guide the house, give none occasion to the adversary to speak reproachfully.'

Who is this adversary that Timothy speaks of? The adversary of woman? Why, Christianity itself.

The women who appear in the New Testament are mainly occupied with washing Jesus's feet with spikenard and cooking meals. Jesus appointed only male disciples. Jesus was a Rabbinic Jew, after all. If Jesus had wanted women to baptise others, he would have been baptised by his mother. If Jesus wanted a female Rock on which to found the eternal See he would have chosen his Aunt Lizzie.

Jesus didn't want a church of human beings, he wanted a football team – eleven players with Judas in reserve.

Who is God? The question occurs to every thinking child, boy and girl.

God is father. God is King. God is Lord. God is shepherd.

God is not mother. Not sister. Not Queen. Not Woman.

The result is the invisible slave at the washtub, in subjection for all the centuries. She is in sexual, political, personal and intellectual limbo, denied a soul or a proper place in the world. Because of the theft of a two-bit apple and her thrusting of the entire human race out of the Garden of Eden, she must suffer in silence. The only Edenic state she is offered is the institution of matrimony, to love and to cherish for as long as ye both shall stand the sight of each other.

But the _____ (insert name) demands

the sweeping away of this mass of superstitious accretion, this barnacle-growth of the spirit politic. The wrangling of schoolmen, the precepts of theologians, the pomposities of 'celibate' priests, in reality fornicators and drunkards. The main point is, we have had enough. We are tired of suffering under the pitiful creeds of men like Augustine, who lived with his mother till he was thirty-five. We regard him with wry amusement.

The original supreme deity was the female principle – Sophia (Wisdom). And so, a word to the wise, to all priests, prophets, popes: 'Out with the new, in with the old!'

Margaret is never anything less than stimulating.

A little editing, I thought, might be required here and there in the matter of industrial politics. I have always held that if the total revenues generated by menial workers were compared to the total revenues generated by brain-workers, the brain-workers would be found to produce an overwhelmingly greater amount *per capita*. This, in fairness, would indicate that factory-hands and miners should be paid *less* than they are now, not more. However, there is no arguing with Margaret on this. And while concurring with her general views on Christianity I regretted her rather elastic view of Christ himself, since it seemed to me that in his teachings he advocated nothing but a sane, natural and wholesome approach toward sex life. All in all, though, apart from the letters, news and calls to industrial sabotage, a very welcome contribution.

Birth Control Monthly was now nearing the point where I could consider publication. I could write much of the first issue myself, if need be. I therefore set the date for 1 January 1926.

XVIII

MR ELIOT

The last day of November began with a ritual
acquired in childhood and re-stimulated I suppose
by Margaret's letter: a perusal of Butler's *Lives of
the Saints for Every Day in the Year*. I discovered what I
had already suspected, that it was St Andrew's Day.
Father Butler had this to say about the saint:

> After suffering a cruel scourging at Patrae in
> Achaia, he was left, bound by cords, to die
> upon a cross. When St Andrew first caught
> sight of the gibbet on which he was to die, he
> greeted the precious wood with joy. 'O good
> cross!' he cried, 'made beautiful by the limbs
> of Christ, so long desired, now so happily
> found! Receive me into thy arms and present
> me to my Master, that He Who redeemed
> me through thee may now accept me from
> thee.' Two whole days the martyr remained
> hanging on this cross alive, preaching, with
> outstretched arms from this chair of truth, to
> all who came near, and entreating them not
> to hinder his passion.[10]

I do not know why I mention it, except that among
the usual postbag I received a communication from
no less a person than Mr T.S. Eliot.

I had, I confess, always regarded Mr Eliot's

___
10 It seems a little hard to reserve special deprecation for one's
rescuers.

poetry to be of little merit – obscure, over-experimental and probably rather damaging. His letter, however, did not mention poetry:

Dear Dr Haldane,

I write with some trepidation, in the hope that you might be able to spare me some of your valuable time. I know you have helped many thousands of others – many, I imagine, with cases far more serious than my own.

The problem relates to my wife Vivien. Since we married in 1915 she has suffered from numerous mental health problems, including migraines, depression and neuralgia. Her behaviour is often quite unpredictable. As an example of the latter, she has recently taken to carrying a joke knife concealed in her underclothing. During a special luncheon last Thursday with Duncan Grant and Vanessa Bell, I was in the act of carving the joint when she rose from her chair, looked at Mrs Bell, and announced: 'My husband is carving the meat, and now I am going to carve you.' She then produced the knife and stabbed Mrs Bell in the forehead. Mrs Bell took it remarkably calmly, only raising a finger in meditative silence to the putative wound, while Vivien shrieked with insane laughter; Doris, our maid, who is well used to this sort of thing, rushed in and sat on her face, since it seems to calm her, though, as Doris says, 'she does nip so.'

The doctors however continue to find

nothing physically wrong with her. The latest medic, a German, prescribed a regular injection of animal glands. After Vivien had left the consulting room in tears he looked at me meaningfully and asked how long we had been married. I replied ten years. He pursed his lips and said, 'When I prescribe animal glands I am thinking of a particular type of animal gland. You may be the only suitable donor.' I must have looked puzzled because he continued, 'This gland is very important for marital relations, and must be injected regularly. Do I make myself clear?' I replied certainly, whatever he thought was best.

I am afraid that since then whatever they were planning to give her has not worked, and although I feel the trouble may lie partly (or even wholly) in the sexual or gynaecological sphere, I have no idea what, if anything, to do.

Is there anything you feel you might suggest?

Yours very sincerely,
Thomas Eliot

I replied immediately as follows:

Dear Mr Eliot,

Thank you for your letter. You may be correct in that the problem lies partly or wholly in the sphere of sex relations (I am afraid I dislike the word 'sexual' – it has a rather slimy ring).

There is a proverb in Japanese that says that as the years of married life pass, the woman wants more and more of what the man is less and less able to give her, and which he himself had previously taught her to demand.[11] It seems likely, given the advice of your physician as you report it, and the fact that she appears to be vying for your attention to a certain extent, that she may be suffering from sex deprivation. One common reaction to this circumstance would be for her to seek self-stimulus, and this of course is very damaging and may lead to nervous problems, including the ones you describe and several scores of others. I would recommend, for her, prostatic and orchitic extract, to make up for the secretions she may be missing as a result of less frequent intercourse. However, a surer route would be for you yourself to provide what she appears to need.

If you can get copies of my books *Wedded Love* and *Enduring Passion* and pass them to your wife as well as reading them yourself, you may find them useful.

With every good wish,

Amber Haldane

PS I am planning a new periodical which will publish the best in poetry and prose and address current issues of burning importance, for example (at random) eugenics and birth

---

11 Japanese proverbs tend to have more clauses than our own.

control. Would you be interested in contributing a short poem to be included in the first issue? It would be an enormous honour for the magazine, and, of course, its editor.

PPS Also try either or both of Fellowe's Syrup of Hypophosphites and Valentine's Meat Juice.

Mr Eliot replied a few days later as follows:

Dear Dr Haldane,

Thank you very much for your kind advice. I will consider it carefully, and try to get some of the substances you mention.

As for poetry, I am flattered by your request and will try to write something for your magazine. I have little experience of writing about eugenics or birth control, however, tending to concentrate on themes such as the void at the heart of existence, the hollow sham of our civilisation and its institutions, etc., none of them ever very popular at the bank, I remember.

Your magazine and its evident purpose remind me of an experience in my earlier career, before coming here to Faber and Gwyer. It was not always easy to get poetry published, and I was doing the rounds of the little magazines: *The Little Review*, *The Small Review*, *The Minuscule Review*, etc., as well as *Vortex*, *Blast*, *Counterblast*, *Disruption*, *Dystopia*, *Discharge*, etc., and, on one occasion, *Midwives'*

Gazette, by mistake. Strangely, on this particular occasion, alone of all the others, *Midwives' Gazette* responded. It seemed they liked my little 'Nocturne', which featured a desultory conversation in a brickyard between two crones:

Yes there was blood
And mucus
And an offensive odour
After that I remember nothing…

A note accompanying payment commented that 'this is the kind of Thing that we are looking for. We need more of this type of thing as it is benificial (sic) to our readers to arm themselves beforehand for the rigours of childbirth. Please send more if you have it, yours, the Editor.' As a result I wrote off with some pieces to *Midwives' Gazette*, *Mother and Baby*, *Your Baby*, *Nursing Times* and *Top Tips for Mums*, but it seems I miscalculated: all the pieces came straight back, I suspect because most were in Greek or Italian.

Your admirer,
Tom Eliot

I replied as follows:

Dear Mr Eliot,

I am greatly pleased that you wish to contribute something. I look forward to it very much. *Midwives' Gazette* is very forward-looking, I agree. I have always admired your poetry, particularly the one with the camel in it, if you recall it.

Yours truly,
Amber Haldane

Dear Dr Haldane,

I think the one you mean might be my piece 'The Journey of the Magi' – it begins 'A cold coming we had of it,/Just the worst time of the year…' It is my only poem that mentions camels.

If you can use the little piece below please do not hesitate.

Limitation of Birth

When will there be an end of it, the insistent thumping
Of feet, the drumming of heels
In celebration of a birth, or of a death?
Or at night, the creak of dry springs?

I spoke to the landlord of these things
And others, meeting him by chance outside
Baker's Chop House in the afternoon
His eye glassy as a dead camel's.

'They are not like us,' he said,
'You see sir, it's the artistic temperament.
We ordinary folk must learn
To make allowances for artists.'
By the back door, in the rank ailanthus of the yard,
I paused once more.
Where would be the end?

'I'd be grateful if you'd keep it down,' I said
This time to the husband.
He made vague statement in reply
Then offered vaguer explanation
By saying what he had not meant
Refusing to elaborate further
Saying he had said enough
Or rather had avoided all
That he had wanted to avoid –

Or perhaps had failed to say
What he in fact had never wanted
And did not feel, and did not care
A scrap about; or rather had
Perhaps at least not failed to not
Avoid not saying or failing to say
Anything at all.

My very best regards,
Tom Eliot

Dear Mr Eliot,

I was enormously pleased to receive your poem. Now you have two poems with camels in them. I should have told you before that I too am a published poet, but I was too shy, I suppose. My latest collection is available from the Windmill Press.

Years ago I mapped out my career: a third was to consist of service to science, a third of service to humanity, and a third of service to literature. I am now entering the literary phase. During a lifetime spent in the public eye, teaching and attempting to improve the lives of women, I have found that all along the profoundest truths have been the ones which escaped scientific analysis.

How do you personally compose poems? I usually find that the words arrive almost fully-formed in my head, sometimes during sleep, and I simply wake up, snatch up a pen and paper, and scribble them down as fast as I can. I often have no idea what they are about. They seem to come, not from personal experience, but from the ancestral race memory, the storehouse of human emotion. I am an imperfect tool of a finer vibration beyond myself, a radiant realm distant from my conscious understanding.

(By the way this correspondence, in the event of my death and its acquisition by the British Library, will be protected from unlicensed publication by the eighty-year rule, and as I expect to live to at least 120, you have no cause for concern.)

May I attach a very brief sample of my work? It is of course not to be compared with yours in any way at all, but your comments would be much appreciated. Walter de la Mare once said of my work that 'the question is not "is it any good?" since that question is answered definitively by the work itself at a casual glance – but "can the quality of this work entirely be believed?"'

Here it is:

Lay

Wingèd spirit
Thou impregnatest me
With celestial light
Unearthly muse
Thou appearest now
In vision bright
Thou facilitatest
My vernal dreams
When life pours out
In rippling streams
Thou penetratest
My temporal care
For thee alone
I let down my hair
By fireside
Where I am bare
Hot gushes
Of passion rare
Thou depositest
In my roseate lair
Wingèd spirit

Yours very truly,
Amber

Dear Amber,

Thank you for your extraordinary poem. I must look out for more of your work. In answer to your question, I find that I compose poetry best when in Switzerland. Another strategy is to have a list of words to use, such as, in my own case, water, rock, dry, sand, dark, fire, broken, hollow, rank, dead, light, dream, stone, dull and so on.

Yours,
Tom Eliot

XIX

A TYPICAL INTERVIEW

The date of the first publication of *Birth Control Monthly* was now less than a month away, and I was pleased to reflect that it would be graced by the work of the two greatest poets writing in English today. At the same time it would include a contribution from the world's second most famous birth controller (Margaret) and greatest nearly-posthumous sexologist (Dr Ellis), with possible further contributions from our greatest science-romance writer (H.G.), our greatest maritime poet (Mr Masefield) and one of our boldest experimental psychologists (Dr Reich). Even if the latter three contributions did not materialise, I had more than enough material from my own pen to make up the first issue, which, with news and advertisements and so on, would be pleasingly substantial. I had rather given up hope of Mr Gandhi.

Naturally my own contribution would focus on contraception: its theory, history and practice. At the Clinics our rule was always to supply contraception without condition or qualification, and to impress on women the absolute *necessity* of contraceptive measures in cases where there was any racial taint, such as congenital tuberculosis, venereal disease, heart disease, kidney disease of any type, epilepsy, leprosy, diabetes, alcoholism, marked feeble-mindedness, or any history of puerperal insanity, eclampsia, toxaemias, albuminuria, or caesarian section within the last two years; less serious conditions indicating that further pregnancy might not be socially appropriate would include poor eyesight, poor hearing, lameness, 'oddness', excessive shyness or confidence, rudeness, etc.

I was at the Clinic in Whitfield St one morning in early December, preparing some remarks along these lines for the leading article, when a couple arrived. The pair were both fairly young, dressed in their 'best': he in an overcoat, navy-blue suit and shirt, though without tie, a pleasant-enough looking young man, possibly the owner of a small garage; she, well-formed and attractive, attired in a light brown skirt and jacket and an elderly fox-fur stole which gave off a strong odour of camphor, and with peroxide curls under a beaded hat.

'We came in last week and got fixed up,' the young man blurted out as soon as they had sat down, 'but she don't think it's going to work.'

'I didn't say that,' said the young woman, looking at the floor.

'Well, what is it then?' the young man demanded of her. There was a silence. He turned to me. '*You* talk to 'er.'

The young woman found her tongue. 'I've got the cap,' she said, 'but I don't see why that means I 'ave to *do* it all the time.'

'She won't 'ave erogamic union,' the young man said crossly.

'I see.'

'I tried telling 'er,' the young man continued, 'I said to 'er, this is one of the greatest and one of the most racially vital questions which arise in this sphere.'

'Yes.' I looked at the young woman. 'May I ask which cap size you were fitted with?'

'I dunno.'

'Is it comfortable?'

The young woman shrugged.

'What contraceptive measures were you accustomed to take, if any, before last week?'

'Jumping an' that.'

'You mean running, lifting, jumping and so on after coitus?'

'Yes.'

'Anything else?'

'No.'

'I see. And how often would you say you were having intercourse?'

'Since Ethel come along we 'aven't 'ardly done it at all,' said the young man, 'And the running and jumping and carrying on don't work, it's bloody silly, excuse me, but it used to get on my nerves, so she says, "In that case I won't do it."'

'And how old is Ethel now?' I asked the girl.

'Four.'

I regarded the young man. 'Would I be correct in thinking that in the past few years you have begun to notice that you have been feeling "queer" and fidgety, if not actually irritable? That you have nocturnal emissions which tend to debilitate you?'

'Maybe,' replied the young man guardedly.

'And you,' I asked the young woman. 'I imagine you too are feeling "off colour" occasionally. You may be feeling some irritability, noticing physical signs of ageing in yourself, fits of anger, oedemas, suspicions of your husband's fidelity, and so on?'

'I don't know about any of that.'

'I see. Well, in any case I am afraid that the conclusions are fairly clear. You are both suffering from a deficit in the nutritive fluids obtained from each other during coitus.'

'Didn't I tell you about the fluids?' roared the young man at his wife. He turned back to me, enraged. 'I told 'er about the bloody fluids!'

'Keep your blimmin' fluids to yourself!' shrieked the girl, snatching at her hat and fox-fur and rushing for the door. She slammed the latter after her, causing the fresh willow-blue curtain and curtain rail in the window to drop with a bang.

The young man watched through the uncurtained window as his wife hurtled across the road. He then regarded me in silent appeal, raising both his hands and letting them fall to his lap. We sat for a moment.

'Well,' I said. 'Rest assured, this is not an unusual case in itself. Many wives are prone to react in this way. I will give you some medicine to help, to be taken by both of you. However, this will not immediately solve the problem, only remedy the symptoms. The important thing to realise is that the restrained and sacramental rhythmic performance of the marriage rite of physical union throughout the whole of married life is an act of supreme value in itself, separate and distinct from its value in the procreation of children.'

'*I* know! I *told* 'er that!'

Such a scene was, I am afraid, quite typical. It was a common belief among the working classes that running, lifting, dancing, jumping, coughing, bouncing, walking, leaping, trampolining (on patent trampolines), stretching, hopping, skipping (with patent ropes) and vaulting were effective post-coital contraceptive measures. Husbands, who at that stage in the marital act were ready to lapse into a post-orgasmic torpor, were often understandably irritated by these performances.

And it was true that working-class women were often less inclined to consent willingly to the marital act than women of other classes. Thinking that they had 'done their duty' in the genesis of numerous offspring, they often became difficult and 'obstinate', presenting at the Clinic with no interest whatever in sex activity, an attitude which their husbands understandably regarded with disfavour.

I was engaged in writing a few notes on the subject for my article when I heard the young man clear his throat.

'So what am I supposed to do?' he asked.

I regarded him a little impatiently. 'Well, she is after all your wife. Close the garage and go somewhere together.'

'Garage?'

'A sunshiny region in the south of France, perhaps, where you can rekindle your mutual passion. Take the matter into your own hands.'

The young man stood up. 'I bloody have to,' he said.

XX

A GIFT

On Christmas Eve of 1925 I received a letter from Havelock Ellis:

My dear Dr Haldane,

Golden sunlight; fresh breezes; a delicate carpet of fallen leaves. These are the only things left to us. But they are all, all.

You have doubtless heard of our recent difficulties. We buried the bodies of Professor Keppel and his daughter in the grounds of the little deserted temple close by, with its grove of cryptomerias. Frau Keppel and her son have departed for the mainland, as has Mrs Assistant Professor Tanaka, with the body of her husband.

The three of us that remain, that is, myself, Françoise and the brilliantined young man, have spent the last several weeks with the local inhabitants of the island. Their rough dwellings of bamboo were largely unaffected by the earthquake, and we have attempted to replicate their construction up on the hill. The sanitary arrangements the people favour here are primitive, but make up for that with some points of interest which I plan to expand into a monograph at a future date.

We intend to remain here, in part because I have sold my family home in Shropshire, its seventeen-acre estate, messuages, dairy business etc. in order to pay for our residence on the island. Accommodation is expensive in Japan.

Although the brilliantined young man was at first feared hurt in the earthquake, he later walked from the wreckage entirely unharmed. As luck would have it, he had spent the night sitting up in the orgone accumulator. When a beam fell on top of it, its sturdy construction of alternating layers of organic and metallic material was able to absorb the blow, simultaneously throwing the door open. Upon the removal of the beam and other debris the brilliantined young man emerged, his person and his composure perfectly intact.

After the bodies were recovered, the work of salvage was undertaken, and we managed to retrieve most of our furniture, books, clothing, utensils and so on, which we put into storage under a temporary canopy.

The orgone accumulator was also recovered, largely undamaged except that the door now does not close properly. We have stored it temporarily in the interior of the nearby temple, where it can now be seen in the gloom by the small statue of Buddha on its pedestal.

The brilliantined young man had spent most or all of his time in the orgone accumulator during our first months on the island, and in fact continues to do so, having fitted an internal latch. Whenever Françoise and I want to get in, he is already there. So we are looking forward greatly to Dr Reich's arrival in the New Year.

I wish to thank you for the food parcel and the supplementary supplies from Professor Fujii in Kyoto. I had never tried Valentine's Meat Juice. I expected a taste rather like gravy or Bovril, but it is quite sweet and rather pungent, is it not? I am afraid I drank it all at once, despite or perhaps because of the instruction on the label, and as a result felt rather odd.

I think you would be greatly taken with our new and improved 'native' accommodations. They are in Japanese style, light and strong in construction, the interiors so arranged that several rooms can be thrown into one by sliding back large dividing screens.

We sincerely hope you will find time from your campaigning work to visit us.

With sincere affection,
Havelock Ellis
Sekkusu-shima Island

PS I enclose a message and small gift from the brilliantined young man, who I feel echoes the sentiments in my last paragraph.

The gift mentioned was a tiny stone, not much bigger than a button, perfectly round and polished, but otherwise unadorned and uncarved. I recognised it immediately. It was rosy amber, a very rare form of amber created by the fossilised roseate sap of ancient trees. It was the most exquisite thing

– a drop of the world's translucent blood, from the days before flowering plants had appeared among the ferns of the primaeval forest. The stone could only have been chosen by someone with knowledge of my deep love for this rose-gold substance, embodying as it did for me all my affinity with ancient things. Accompanying it was a message written in ink, with a brush, on a torn piece of rice paper. It read as follows:

> I thank you for your gift, and salute you as a poet.

XXI

NEW YEAR'S EVE 1925;
A CONTRIBUTION FROM H.G.

New Year's Eve was a time spent, to my great pleasure, with the Eliots, Bosie, H.G. and Dr Harvard at
Westbury Park.

The occasion was not, of course, just the beginning of the new year, but the night before the first
publication of *Birth Control Monthly*, a mere four
months since the germ of the idea had been plant-
ed in my mind by H.G.'s telephone call.

H.G. had finally produced a story – entitled 'Re-
birth' – which he had sent me five days earlier. It
was, as I expected, an adroit performance, though
almost certainly very damaging. It was not in any
case in time for the first issue. I give it in the Appen-
dix for those interested.

Around eight o'clock H.G. himself arrived, followed by Mr and Mrs Eliot. Vivien Eliot, a woman
in her late thirties, wore a flowing dress striped with
iridescent colours; her dark auburn hair was long
and soft, and around her neck and in her ears, gold
glittered. Her beauty was startling. But when she
came to shake hands, with lips parted in greeting,
her eyes were elsewhere. And all that evening it
was plain that a secret pain inhabited her and set
her apart from the company. The symptoms of
deprivation from prostatic and orchitic fluid were, I
feared, only too apparent.

Eliot, a tall, slightly bowed figure, seemed almost
spectral beside his wife. His eyes were perhaps his

most notable feature. They were large and doe-like, with long brown lashes.

John collected Bosie from the station shortly after the Eliots arrived, and by nine we were all sitting at dinner in the Blue Drawing Room where D'Arblay had courted Fanny Burney and Germaine de Staël had toyed, not unproductively, with Louis de Narbonne. We decided to go ahead without Dr Harvard, who was late, and began with the soup, my own invention – chicken and hypophosphite consommé.

'Who is this Dr Harvard?' asked Bosie as we began.

'He is a rather lonely young man who does not have any family here,' I replied. 'A scientist.'

'Oh, a scientist,' said Bosie, for whom all such were equally reprehensible. He glowered at H.G. across the table. 'You can get some ideas for your books, Mr Wells. Perhaps he is doing experiments to make diamonds out of old encyclopaedias.'

'Funny you should mention that,' said H.G. 'I am not planning to make diamonds, but I do have a project concerning encyclopaedias. The project is, one might say, a global encyclopaedia. Ultimately it would be unrecognisable as an encyclopaedia in the conventional sense.'

'Naturally,' said Bosie.

'It would in the final analysis be a bank for all world knowledge and opinion, housed in a single large repository, and continuously added to and updated. All the data would be available to members of the public.'

'A public library,' I said after a moment.

H.G. nodded. 'Yes, in a sense. The collection of information I have in mind would be compiled in a central clearing house like a gigantic typing pool, located anywhere in the world. Anyone who wanted to submit any piece of information, a word, a page, an article, would simply walk in to the front desk and hand it over, whence it would be carried to a pool of teletypers. You've heard of a teleprinter. The article would be sent by teleprinter down the wires to every subscriber, anywhere in the world. The subscribers of course would have teleprinters of their own. It would come out automatically at the other end. In the future the whole thing could possibly be scanned through some sort of viewer, perhaps using an electronic Braun tube.'

'It seems a rather odd thing to have in an ordinary household,' I put in. 'There would be an element of disruption to domestic peace, surely, with such a thing chattering away constantly in the corner?'

'Magazines and newspapers would be created and distributed in the same way. One wouldn't buy a copy every week, or every day. They would be constantly updated on a rolling basis.'

'It is ingenious,' I said, 'but I wonder about the wisdom of letting anyone who wished to do so to submit an article. Your encyclopedia would soon be nothing but lies and pornography.'

'Then it would reflect our civilisation of 1925 rather well,' said Vivien Eliot, tipping the contents of her wine glass into her mouth. 'A comprehensive index of our own depravity.' She glanced at her husband. 'What do you think, dear?' There was a pause while Eliot endeavoured to find an answer. Allowing him no more than two seconds, she turned to Bosie. 'May I ask what you are working on at the moment, Lord Alfred?'

'I am writing a biography of Wilde,' said Bosie. 'I have been instructed by my publishers to produce something that children and young people can read without moral peril.'

'Is it to be published soon?' she asked.

'I have not written more than two sentences.'

'Well, we certainly need more books like that,' said Mrs Eliot. 'You would be the counter to the depravity I spoke of. There is no use relying on the modern writer for this. For the modern writer, there is only birth, copulation and death.'

Eliot smiled, a genial ghost.

'Do I detect a quotation?' I asked. 'Perhaps from Mr Eliot's poetry?'

'I am afraid I am largely ignorant of modern poetry,' Vivien Eliot replied, re-filling her glass. 'I find it difficult to read.'

'I too,' said Bosie, glancing at Eliot. 'With all due deference to Mr Eliot, I must say I feel that the modern experiment is a cul-de-sac.'

'Yes, I have heard that said,' remarked Eliot.

'Where can one go next,' said Bosie, 'when one has turned one's back on rhyme and metre, not to say sense and beauty? What of the great subjects of our age – war, human progress, spiritual values?'

'I find at the moment I seem to be writing mainly about camels,' replied Eliot.

'Ah yes, I understood as much from Dr Haldane. What is it you find attractive about the camel?'

'I do not find it attractive, as such. I simply find it intrudes.'

'It intrudes?'

'Not literally, of course.'

'And that is enough to make it a subject for verse?'

'In my opinion,' I said quickly, 'there is no modern or traditional poetry. There is only the one poetry, and, I maintain, only the one subject – love between man and woman. Erogamic love, in which human nature finds its greatest fulfillment.'

'I am afraid I disagree,' said Bosie.

'May I ask about the interesting word you used – "erogamic"?' enquired Eliot.

'It is a word I have coined for the purpose of crystallising what I believe is a vital idea. It designates that noble flower of the duity of human life, the coming together of man and woman in three planes, mental, physical and spiritual.'

'So, a trinity enclosed within a duity,' observed H.G., 'which makes six altogether.'

'The erogamic life,' I continued, 'is the elevation of the physiological aspects of sex which we share with the animals. It is thus not merely what some call "sexual" life, but the evolved interplay of man and woman. We can leave the ugly word "sexual" to those who still delight in the soiled and bedraggled echoes of the centuries. The world has rightly sickened of talk about "sexual" matters.'

'That seems a paradox of quite magnificent proportions,' H.G. said.

'Well, I am with you, Mrs Haldane,' said Vivien Eliot, looking at me with dislike. 'These men care nothing for what you have just said. On the one hand we have the great Mr Wells, who has visions of the future. On the other we have my husband, who has visions of the past. And opposite me is a poet of great stature who tells us he cannot write of the only thing that he cares about. None of them seem able to live in the here and now, to pluck the flower of life, as you say. This is the rose garden from which they are exiled.'

'Just a moment,' said Eliot. 'Did you bring my commonplace book?'

'Here. I have already pencilled it in for you.'

'Oh.'

'Do you really think so?' asked H.G. 'I find it is when I have visions of the future that I am most conscious of the here and now. For example, this morning, at breakfast, I began dreaming of the year thirty million. Frightened the living daylights out of me.'

The maid brought in the main course, another recipe of mine, oyster and tangerine hotpot.

There was a lull while those present attacked their plates.

'Well,' said H.G. at length, addressing a piece of pith on the end of his fork, 'I must say I welcome all you young poets from the Americas making your home here. You and Mr Pound and so on. It is exactly what we need. I am a wholehearted supporter of modernism in all its forms. I only wonder what attracted you here. I rather fancy that if I were a young man now, I would be going in the opposite direction.'

Eliot again appeared briefly to struggle for

utterance, running a forefinger in a controlled fashion across the tablecloth as he did so. 'My father was the president of the Hydraulic-Press Brick Company in St Louis, Missouri,' he said. 'He encouraged me to strive for high achievement in life, and to live up to family standards of success.'

'Mr Eliot came here to study at Oxford, of course,' I put in.

'Yes, indeed,' said Eliot. 'I have many happy memories of Merton, and it was there' – he turned to Vivien Eliot with a sickly grin – 'it was while I was at Oxford that I met my wife. But to answer your question, Mr Wells: my father, indeed my whole family, are strict Unitarians. Unitarianism is not a denomination that is particularly well known or represented in this country. It stresses the importance of man's faculties of reason and rejects original sin. Unitarians believe that God is present in every individual and throughout the natural world. I am afraid I found it increasingly repugnant.'

'You wished to escape,' I said. 'I understand. I…'

'Don't you believe it,' interrupted Vivien Eliot. 'To wish for escape is to wish for what is better. To wish for escape is to seek freedom from misery, from captivity. Misery and captivity are my husband's natural habitat.'

'Doubtless they are,' said Eliot, attempting a laugh.

Mrs Eliot stared at her plate. 'You mentioned just now the word you have coined, Mrs Haldane. I too have coined a word. Uxoriphobia. It denotes fear and hatred of one's wife.' She gestured with her glass at Eliot, sloshing him slightly. 'Tom here is an uxoriphobe. "The Waste Land" is all about me, you see. How I smell and how I taste, and how revolted he is by me. It is full of Tom's hatred. But Ezra cut out all the best bits. The bits that describe…'

'Please, dear.'

'Don't "please" me!' she shrilled.

'Forgive me. All I was going to say was that if I suffer from anything it is panphobia, fear of everything. My uxoriphobia, if any − I hope there is none − is a department of my panphobia.'

'So I am a department!'

'Please, dear!'

'I said, don't "please" me!'

'No, of course not.'

'I have never gone in for poetry,' said H.G. 'I don't know why. I have gone in for everything else. Perhaps I should give it a try.'

'Do you think at your age that is wise?' asked Bosie.

'I don't see why not. Literature is undergoing a revolution. It seems obvious, to me at any rate, that the days are numbered in which literature will be produced by individuals. All books in the future will be written by machine. And poetry, it seems fairly obvious, will be the first on the list.'

'Nonsense.'

'Consider a specimen of verse as written by Newbolt. It has a regular verse structure, lines of a set length containing a certain number of feet, and it rhymes AA BB CC DD and so on. Such a thing has a great deal of mathematics in it.'

'Your ignorance is quite ridiculous,' said Bosie. 'I say that with no malice. If there is any automation to be done, your novels seem to me to be more suitable candidates. Throw the words "ant", "giant", "time", "travel", "fantastic", "island", "reptilian" and so on into a sack and jumble them up, then take them out one at a time with a few selected conjunctions. *Et voilà!*'

'You've got quite a few of my favourite words there,' said H.G. 'If I didn't know better, I'd almost begin to suspect you'd read my books.'

'Have you heard about the island experiment of Dr Ellis in Japan?' I asked Eliot, changing the subject. 'It is in some respects quite remarkable.'

'My husband is already an island,' observed Mrs Eliot.

'Yes, what do you think to that?' said H.G. to Eliot. 'That is the perfect antidote to our diseased civilisation. No motor-cars. No gramophones. Nothing to eat but the fruit as it grows.'

'And throbbing native drums,' said Bosie, 'offering sacrifice to savage gods.'

'Yes,' said Eliot meditatively. 'Yes. It sounds most attractive.'

'I will book your passage immediately,' said Vivien Eliot to her husband. 'On your own. One way.'

'I am sure Mr Eliot would never wish to leave his adopted country,' said Bosie.

'I am sure he *would*,' said Mrs Eliot with offensive emphasis, craning her jaw at Bosie over the table. The tips of her coils of red hair, shining richly in the candlelight, lightly caressed the gravy on her plate.

'Please, dear,' said Eliot again.

'Please, dear! Please, dear!' screamed Vivien Eliot. 'I don't know why I don't murder you! I will, too! I will murder you!' She took up a fork and advanced on Eliot's unresisting throat.

'Stop!' cried a voice.

In the doorway Dr Harvard stood framed in light. He was dressed in an immaculate grey double-breasted suit, a viridian silk tie with matching handkerchief and patent-leather shoes shone to a high polish. He walked slowly to the table.

'Zere are very strong electrical forces operating in zis room!' he announced. 'Please stay completely still!'

With cat-like tread he began to circle the guests. Bosie regarded him with alarm, H.G. with delighted fascination; Eliot seemed to have been expecting him. Dr Harvard finally came to rest behind Mrs Eliot, then bent down to her ear, and murmured into the silence of the room: 'I am sensing very strong feelings of orgastic potency emanating from you, Madam.'

With a terrible wail Vivien Eliot rose from her seat, pulling at the tablecloth and bringing down several glasses and a floral arrangement. Then she rushed for the French windows, strove with them, and was gone into the night.

'You bloody great idiot!' shouted Eliot. 'Look what you've done!' He bolted after her.

Dr Harvard seemed quite broken by his success. 'It voss a... a party game of mine,' he stammered.

'Never mind,' said H.G. 'Sit down and have an oyster.'

XXII

BIRTH CONTROL MONTHLY IS PUBLISHED

Brilliantine is a strange substance. It comes as a species of thin white cream, sold in either tube or jar. Out of curiosity I bought some more and this time examined it with more attention. The texture was rather slippery and thin, and it spread quickly and easily through hair. Its scent was unusual, slightly reminiscent of cocoanuts, and with a base perhaps of castor oil or mineral oil. I strongly suspected, from its slight opalescence, that it contained lethicin or possibly butylene glycol, but there were no indications on the packaging one way or the other. Its effect, of course, is to add a natural humectancy to hair, softening it and adding sheen; this would tend to make straight hair flatter and perhaps rather unappealing, but would give body and styling to curlier hair. It seemed likely that the brilliantined young man, as a person of taste, would have this latter type of hair, which, being black, as Dr Ellis had indicated in an earlier letter, would then exhibit a high degree of glossiness.

Shortly after the incidents described above, the Eliots departed, and the evening, without the presence of Mrs Eliot, settled into a more established groove. Bosie became very drunk and attacked H.G. with such high-flown savagery that we failed to notice the passing of midnight, and the arrival of the New Year. Dr Harvard's distress at the incident with Vivien Eliot passed off after an hour or so, and he began telling us more about the plans of Dr

Reich, who was due to arrive in Japan in mid-February. We retired, quite exhausted, at around three a.m. In the morning H.G. left for London fairly early, though not before taking a photograph of Dr Harvard, myself and Bosie standing on the steps of the conservatory.

A week after publication, *Birth Control Monthly* began to enjoy considerable public success.

The first issue, distributed by the Clinics and the Society for Constructive Birth Control, sold out in a week. My first editorial was entitled 'God will have Blood', and read as follows:

> Millions of people throughout the world hunger and thirst for guidance on the pressing problems of the day, and look to the Holy Roman Catholic Church to provide it. They look not only for spiritual enlightenment but also guidance on how they should, with rectitude, conduct their most intimate human relationships.
>
> Trusting in the reality of papal infallibility – which, if it were true, would mean that the Bishop of Rome could never be wrong, not even if he were to become irrecoverably insane and issue any sort of ridiculous edict or encyclical, demanding that his followers dress only in violet robes or wake up at two o'clock in the morning to eat mackerel – these millions ask for clear guidance on the most crucial issue of their lives: the correct manner in which to call forth new souls into the world. 'Is it permissible,' they ask meekly, 'to

regulate fertility during the performance of the sacred act of erogamic union? Especially in cases where mothers are struggling with ill health or are so weakened and bloodied by successive pregnancies that their children are born crippled or feeble-minded? Or where families, and the nation, are so burdened with diseased and sub-par offspring that there is an imminent danger of the rotting and catastrophic collapse of the social fabric?'

'Certainly,' replies the Holy Catholic Church. 'Divine law, as revealed in the Scriptures, does not explicitly condemn birth control. Nowhere did Christ condemn voluntary parenthood by eugenically fit and healthy parents. Nowhere in the New Testament, or the Old, are contraceptive devices specifically anathematised. In fact, primitive versions of them were almost certainly known to the Jews and to all ancient peoples. Nevertheless, the tradition of the Holy Catholic Church, just for no particular reason, is that the use of all artificial preventative methods is unlawful for Christians. This tradition has been observed since earliest times.'

'Then nothing is to be done?'

'My children,' the luminary of the Church responsible for indoctrination might continue, 'the Catholic Church condemns only artificial methods. The Church does not condemn natural methods of family limitation.'

'Oh, good… which particular ones?'

'Ones in which, by the determination of a

period during the natural female cycle where there is no potentiality of fertilisation, male and female may come together in union.'

'So – let us be clear, then – it would not be against the teaching of the Holy Mother Church to adopt methods of preventing conception, as long as those methods did not include the interposition of certain man-made devices between the generative organs of the sexes?'

'Correct.'

'And if those approved methods that avoided any man-made device were so unreliable as to have a failure rate exceeding 50 per cent, then that would still be considered an excellent solution?'

'Quite.'

'I see. Well, thank you for clearing that up.'

'My pleasure.'

So are the little ones advised. And so much misery is brought forth on the face of the earth.

Let us put it rather more strongly: the Church is prepared to sanction contraceptive methods as long as they do not work.

Birth Control Monthly calls for an end to this obscurantism. It is an insult to the minds of all civilised people. The joining of married people in the holy duity of physical union, allowing for healthful interpenetration of fluids and after careful wooing of the female in question, etc., etc., is too important to be regulated by the 'wisdom' of churchmen who might have been capable of giving suitable advice in the early days of Christianity in the era of Roman persecution, when all sorts of abuses were current, such as the provision of entertainments in which giraffes were roasted alive (see Suetonius for details), but who are grotesquely ill-equipped to comprehend the demands of married urban people in the twentieth century who wish to 'do their bit' to avoid racial liquidation. That the act of sex union for normal married people should have its spontaneity trammelled by a cabal of decrepit celibates in a medieval fortress in Italy is to traduce the dignity of the race and to debase the supreme human art, the art of love.

Reviews of the first issue were somewhat mixed, as might be expected in a national press well furnished with Catholics, Jews and their sympathisers. *The Times* was moderately generous, saying that 'the magazine is aimed at healthy persons of the middle classes wishing to avoid an existence dominated by self-shame, and who feel unable to speak of certain delicate matters'; Admiral Sir Percy Stott, writing in the *Daily Telegraph*, noted that 'for the first time it seems possible entirely to eliminate whole sections of the lower orders, and along with them the labour troubles that have been such a blight on settled governance'. *Poetry* welcomed 'an interesting development in the recent camel theme of Mr Eliot'. However, the less intelligent papers, such as the *Standard*, were quick to make cheap points such as

'Dr Haldane is not a medical woman', or 'birth regulation is still a matter of debate', which is obviously not the case. One Mr Aleister Crowley, writing in *The Sackbut*, commented that 'the whole secret of the way of initiation is laid open here... the truth is no longer shrouded in an impenetrable cloak of mystery... the guardians of esoteric knowledge are challenged and the seals of the wells are cracked' – which sounded positive. The *Daily Express* merely remarked that '*Birth Control Monthly* will doubtless receive the recognition it deserves.'

The longest, most energetic and most hostile review came from one Monsignor Dr Isidore Blackwell Garnet, a Catholic priest and physician, the Gynaecological Observer at the Convent of the Sacred Heart, Edinburgh, writing in the *Catholic Inquirer.* I quote it in full:

> The recent publication of a new magazine, ludicrously entitled *Birth Control Monthly*, is a challenge to the instincts of all right-thinking people. Published by Mrs Amber Haldane, it presents to the public a strange farrago of eugenical polemic, poetry and misinformation.
>
> It is incomprehensible that these writings should be tolerated by the Home Secretary. The monstrous campaign led by this doctor of German philosophy is nothing less than an experiment on the poor. Mrs Haldane's avowed aim is to remodel England's racial identity in the image of herself. Well, this will not do. The future direction of the English race is in the hands of God. It is outrageous

that anyone should seek to frustrate God's design for humanity, or question the potential value of any unborn life.

Fortunately the poor themselves do not, in general, support or condone these practices, and in fact use contraceptive methods less than any other segment of the population. But if *Birth Control Monthly* has its way this will change. The nation will be weakened at home and abroad. The future of the Empire is at stake.

As if to extend her pernicious influence to every sphere possible, Mrs Haldane chooses to recommend the most actively harmful contraceptive method known to medical science – that is, the rubber check pessary. Her brand of birth control is an insult to true womanhood, a degradation of the female sex, an incitement to immorality and a danger to health. This is nothing less than the extension of German materialism into the sexual sphere: that self-same philosophical materialism that led, not so recently, to a world war in which 15 million men were slaughtered.

No one can deny the sexual impulse was created for the purpose of procreation. So to extol any other purpose over that original and sacrosanct purpose is to court blasphemy. In the Roman Empire, men were accustomed to recline and gorge themselves with every dainty tidbit their cooks could devise, afterwards vomiting up what they had eaten so they could begin again with renewed appetite. It is this swinishness that the advocates of birth control encourage. The birth controller extols the secondary end over the primary. He seeks to gratify the sex impulse, yet defeats its aim, and so goes against nature, conscience, ethics and God's law.

I decided to sue.

PART TWO

MONDAY

Court Four – more properly the Lord Chief Justice's Court of the King's Bench Division of the High Court in the Strand, London – was packed with a sweaty rabble that would not have disgraced a print by Gillray. The three tiers of the public gallery held a veritable legion of cranks, journalists, polygamists, Catholics, red-faced men – anyone who had ever opened a newspaper, in fact, and many who had never – all of whom were were perspiring and shouting at the tops of their voices. A trio of placards was visible through the long windows:

BIRTH CONTROL IS MURDER
WHITE SLAVERY IN LEATHERHEAD
GERMAN MATERIALISM

The judge, Mr Justice Mummery, sat high up at the rear, under a gleaming downward-pointing sword. Below him in the black-silk-clad legal melée was my own counsel, my solicitor's choice, Mr Patrick Brain.

At nine o'clock a.m., Mr Brain stood up to open the case for the Prosecution. Short, pale, moth-eaten, prematurely bald, havering, stammering, he had a strange, unattractive tuft of hair protruding from his Adam's apple.

'If your Lordship and members of the Jury please,' he began, his voice attempting to still the clamour, 'this is an action for a claim of criminal libel against Monsignor Dr Isidore Blackwell Garnet, the Defendant, on behalf of Dr Amber Haldane, the Plaintiff in this matter.'

The judge rapped his gavel a few times.

'I am obliged to your Lordship,' Mr Brain continued weakly. 'Now, if I may – if I may begin. Well then, let us start with the chief matter in this case. This is a trial for criminal libel – that is, the unlawful publication, in print, of an untruth that may cause harm – against the person of Dr Amber Haldane. Now: many of the members of the jury will have heard of the work of Dr Haldane. Even those who have never visited the Clinic which she founded at her own expense in London, nor read any of her books, nor heard her speak, and in fact even those of you who have led instead an entirely blameless existence' – he narrowed his mouth as if aware that something had gone awry with his train of thought – 'even those, I say, could hardly have failed to have heard of her work. She has led what many people would agree is a very valuable life in the promotion of the theory and practice of what has come to be known as birth control.'

He paused with an attempt at gravitas, spoiled by his shuffling from one foot to the other.

'I will read out to you the passage in which the libel consists. It appeared first in a newspaper called the *Catholic Inquirer*, the overt purpose of which is to promulgate the doctrines of the Roman Church, which are, as you will know, opposed to all forms of birth control. This then is the libel. I have it here… just one moment… Where has it gone?… Ah yes. These are the passages complained of, marked in red. You cannot see them marked in red; they are only marked in red on my copy. But you do not have a copy, I realise. So I will read them out.'

Mr Brain raised a wilting sheaf of papers in the direction of the Jury. I noticed that there were animal hairs on his gown.

'The first passage complained of,' he continued, 'is this: "It is incomprehensible that these writings should be tolerated by the Home Secretary. The monstrous campaign led by this doctor of German philosophy is nothing less than an experiment on the poor." I jump forward in the article at this point, to arrive at the second passage, which is as follows: "As if to extend her pernicious influence to every sphere possible, Mrs Haldane chooses to recommend the most actively harmful contraceptive method known to medical science – that is, the rubber check pessary." These words this gentleman, Dr Monsignor Isidore Blackwell Garnet, must justify.

'Now, who is Dr Haldane? I will tell you. She is a lady of remarkable talent from a family of remarkable talent. Her father, before his death, was the archaeologist John Mullender Haldane. Her mother was a leading light in the Rational Dress Society, whose quarterly magazine was once edited by no less a person than Mr Oscar Wilde, that same Mr Oscar Wilde who was tried in this very court, where we are sitting now – where you are sitting now – and was sentenced to two years' imprisonment, with hard labour.'

Loud laughter broke over Mr Brain, who seemed mystified by it, as if it were an exhibit brought in from another trial. Among the many raucous mouths was one woman whose calling card was a single, ear-splitting shriek.

The Lord Chief Justice frowned.

'But that is of no importance to this case, I merely mention it,' Mr Brain hurried on. 'Now, from an early age, this lady, Dr Haldane, the Plaintiff, has interested herself in numerous researches of all kinds, in minerals, and coals, and so on and so forth. In pursuance of these researches she has travelled all around the world, visited America, Russia, Finland, Africa, New Zealand and Japan, and been welcomed as an honoured guest, except I believe in America, where they took exception to something she had written.'

Loud laughter.

'But elsewhere she was received with the greatest of all courtesy at the highest levels of society. Now, in the course of her studies, she desired to extend her researches to Germany, having attained every qualification here that it was possible to attain. You see from that what a distinguished figure she is. So she went to Munich, where she studied for two years and learned the German language, receiving the distinction of becoming the youngest Doctor of Philosophy of that country at the age of twenty-five. She is in addition a fellow of the Linnaean Society and a fellow of the Royal Society of Literature. Yet, with all those distinctions to choose from, what did the Defendant light upon to describe her? He said she was a "Doctor of German Philosophy". Never mind that the title of philosopher was one that she could never claim. That is, never mind that this Doctorate was not in philosophy. Never mind all that. No, this was an attempt, pure and simple, to tar her with the German brush, to suggest that she was trying somehow to extend the influence of Germany into the reproductive arena. This imputation of Germanness is not nice – this insinuation that Dr Haldane may have had any other motive other than helping poor women. And I hope that if the Defendant regrets nothing else in this case and wins it entirely, he will at least find it in himself to regret those words.

'Now, let me tell you something else of Dr Haldane. This is by no means the first time she has been in court…' (Laughter) '… which is not to suggest, gentlemen of the Jury, that she is a frequent litigant, quite the contrary. But this may be pertinent to the case at hand. Her first marriage, contracted in 1910, ended in disastrous failure. The cause of that failure was her husband's inability to consummate the criminal act. I mean the conjugal act.' (Laughter.) 'His peculiar physical incapacity in this sphere made her life so wretched that she was forced to pursue a suit of nullity in order to extricate herself from this terrible situation, in which no woman would willingly remain, as I am sure the gentlemen of the Jury can imagine. Dr Haldane's husband was by all accounts a man of strange habits, very probably rendered unfit for marital life by certain acts of careless lasciviousness in his youth.' (A shriek.) 'But we do not need to go into all that. All that needs to be said is that, having obtained a certificate of perfect purity and intactness, which I believe is now in the British Library, she was able to gain satisfaction in the courts in a legal sense, even though her personal happiness was in utter rout and ruin.

'Now I mention this because it was the experience of conjugal misery that led to her later work – the funding of her birth control clinic and the Society for Constructive Birth Control. Thus her work among the poorest of the poor began as a result of this little affair with her husband.' (Laughter.) 'This little matter. Now, what was I going to say next?' (Laughter.) 'Oh yes. I would finally like to draw your attention to a document, a letter that was published as part of the introduction to the book *Wedded Love* by Dr Haldane. A letter received from one Father Xavier St John Montevergine, a priest in the Roman Catholic Church, expressing support for the work of Dr Haldane, though perhaps understandably in rather qualified language, no doubt because of his faith's opposition to any policy of family limitation. Since this book, *Wedded Love*, has been on the *Index Librorum Prohibitorum*, the Roman list of banned books, the letter has been withdrawn from subsequent editions, and no one knows what has happened to Father Xavier. But in the earlier editions this letter appeared. It was sent from 113 Bethel Street, Dublin, on the 21st of December 1917.

'"Dear Dr Haldane," it reads, "many thanks for your invitation to write a preface for your book. I have read it and find much to commend in it. Many of the marital difficulties I encounter in my parish work come from failures of understanding between husband and wife. Your opinions and my own inevitably diverge on several counts, as might be expected. I question your idea that there is a regular fortnightly surge and relapse of female desire, or that working women should take holidays in Alpine regions. Nor can I see any merit in the suggestion that couples who are engaged to be married should be given any idea of what awaits them in the connubial state, since it seems to me that no surer incitement to immorality could be imagined. I also disagree, as you might expect, that husbands and wives should, for purely selfish reasons, indulge in sexual intercourse without bearing children as a consequence. I take a longer view than you, perhaps, feeling that any ill health suffered by the mother of a large family is to be set against the gift, for her potential offspring, of eternal bliss with God after this temporal existence has passed away. To deny any soul an eternity with a loving Deity just because of a varicose vein here or there seems quite wrong. The teaching of the Church, that the destruction of even a single spermatozoon is to be avoided even at the risk of permanently crippling or killing its potential female incubator, seems to me eminently sane and reasonable. And I have many other points of disagreement with you: my thoughts on orgasm alone could cover many pages. All things considered, however, I recognise that your motives are well-intentioned, even though I find your conclusions fundamentally evil. Providing you air these comments in full I am willing that you publish this letter. Believe me, Dr Haldane, I remain, yours very sincerely, Father Xavier St John Montevergine."'

Mr Brain put down his paper, his hand wavering slightly.

'Now, I venture to say,' he continued, 'that from a priest of the Roman Church this is high praise indeed, and expressed despite his obvious fears, which it seems may have been well founded, given his sudden and unexplained disappearance. Yet it is this very same book that the Defence asserts is criminal and obscene. Well! Gentlemen, I feel I can do no more than end these brief opening remarks and call the lady herself to the witness stand. It is she who must satisfy you; it seems to me that anything further I say to you would simply be so much chaff thrown away and wasted.' (Laughter.) 'This case cannot be won by me. I therefore call Dr Amber Haldane.'

I walked briskly to the stand. I had decided on my silver fox-fur coat and a plain dark dress with simple white quaker collar and cuffs, the one that had been so successful in my 1923 appeal trial.

I was the only woman in the main body of the courtroom.

'You are Dr Amber Haldane, of Westbury Park, Dorking?' Mr Brain began. From my slightly closer vantage point I could see the tiny beads of sweat that had formed on the crown of his head.

'Near Dorking, yes,' I replied.

'I have already set out your qualifications, but is it the case that you attended London University, where you won a medal?'

'Yes.'

'And did you then go to Munich to obtain a degree of Doctor of Philosophy?'

'Yes.'

'Since your studies, have you had a considerable amount of experience teaching at universities?'

'Yes.'

'You have had many young men under you?'

'Yes.'

'Is it true that you were married?'

'As a physical fact it was never a marriage. I applied for and was granted a suit of nullity in my marriage because of certain parts of my husband.'

'Parts.'

'Certain parts,' I explained, 'which, because of their lack of certain qualities, made him incapable of the sacramental performance of the marital act.'

'You hold that the marital act is a sacrament?'

'Certainly. The restrained and rhythmic performance of the marital act is the foundation of social happiness, and a sacrament by that fact.'

'Yes…'

'Many young girls who are brought up in ignorance and innocence are all but unaware of the facts of sex life. For the first few years of my marriage I myself was unaware that anything was wrong. It was only later that I came to suspect that there was some abnormality in the marriage.'

'And it was then that you started your campaign for what is called birth control?' Mr Brain asked.

'For wider knowledge of all aspects of marital happiness.'

'Now just a few questions on this campaign of birth control.'

'I do not wish to intervene in your advocacy on my behalf, Mr Brain,' I broke in tactfully, 'which generally seems excellent. But I must point out that the campaign is wider than that of birth control. It relates to a general attempt to promote matrimonial happiness existing between couples. Briefly: it has been my experience that healthy and happy societies depend on healthy and happy homes, and healthy and happy homes depend on knowledge of the normal right experience and relation between husband and wife, which in turn depends on the correct exchange of certain fluids, the acidity or alkalinity…'

'May I stop you there?' Mr Brain said. His irritation was manifest. 'One is anxious, if possible, to keep answers within certain limits. Now, what was your purpose in founding the Mothers' Clinics?'

'To prevent the reckless breeding of the degenerate and defective sections of the population,' I began, 'so as to diminish the number of rotten or semi-feebleminded individuals…'

'Quite, quite,' Mr Brain put in. 'You wished to ameliorate poverty and improve conditions for working mothers and children to foster the growth of a healthier population.'

The Lord Chief Justice, who had not spoken at all up to this point, roused himself from a legal slumber.

'I do not think that that was necessarily implied by the answer just given,' he said in a soupy tone of voice.

'I am obliged to your Lordship, Mr Brain replied, bowing. 'Very well. I will pass from that.' He turned back to face me. 'I dare say you will have noticed that in this case there is the accusation that you are subjecting the poor to experiment?'

'That is why we are here, after all,' I replied.

'Precisely. Have you or your nurses ever conducted experiments on the poor?'

'In no sense.'

'Never fitted experimental contraceptive devices?'

'Never.'

'You mentioned acid. Have you ever used acid?'

'No.'

'Neither *in vitro* or *in vivo*?'

'There is acid in quinine pessaries, but it is of a very weak kind and could not be judged experimentation, since it has been used since time immemorial, for example in the form of citrus juice.'

'That is certainly clear... ah... what about X-rays?'

'X-rays?'

'Yes, have you ever used X-rays?'

'No.'

'You have never used any device that emitted any type of radiation?'

'Never. No sort of poison. My guiding principle is never to put into the vagina anything that you would not put into your own mouth.'

On hearing this sensible piece of advice, and the extremely prolonged laughter that followed it, the Lord Chief Justice looked with distaste at the public gallery, and then at myself, but, apparently unable to decide which party to reprehend, said nothing.

'Yes. Ah... that is eminently clear,' Mr Brain went on. 'Thank you. Ah... now, you have an income from your writing, I understand?'

'A small income.'

'And the Clinics are funded exclusively by you?'

'Exclusively.'

'Do you receive any financial reward from them?'

'None.'

'So there is no financial motive in opening these clinics?'

'No.'

'You could, if you wished, lead a life of ease and comfort in the country doing absolutely nothing?'

'If I wished.'

'Complete leisure.'

'I would probably milk the cow.'

'Quite. But that would be your only duty?'

'Unless I hired a milkmaid, yes.'

'But you do not.'

'I prefer to do it myself. There is only one cow.'

Laughter – though at what, I was unable to see.

'So you have the private means to avoid milking the cow manually, that is, yourself, if you wished, with your own hands, but you prefer to milk it yourself.'

The Lord Chief Justice appeared to decide that reprehending Mr Brain was the appropriate *via media*. 'Please confine yourself to questions, Mr Brain,' he said.

'In that case, let me put that another way,' the counsel for the Prosecution said, his brow corrugating in forensic thought. 'Do you prefer to milk it yourself?'

'Yes. It does not take up much time,' I said.

'Ten minutes or so?'

'You are leading the witness,' the Lord Chief Justice remarked testily.

'I will rephrase the question,' Mr Brain said. 'How long does it take to milk the cow?'

'Ten minutes or so.'

Prolonged laughter.

'Thank you. Well, that is clear. Thank you. I have no further questions.'

Mr Lemmons, the counsel for the Defence, was a pleasing contrast to Mr Brain. Well-formed, with a dark skin and hair, and large, penetrating eyes – I thought he might have had some Spanish ancestry – he put me in mind of the brilliantined young man described so vividly by Dr Ellis. He seemed remarkably at ease.

'Let us examine some issues a little more germane to this case,' he said in a pleasant light baritone. 'Mrs Haldane, are you a prophet of God?'

'I believe God has a message for humanity at this time,' I replied carefully.

'May I have a yes or a no?'

'It is my belief that the Holy Spirit may move any one of us.'

'I repeat my question: are you a prophet of God?'

'In the sense that any one of us may be.'

'Does God personally recommend the check pessary?'

'He recommends what he sees fit,' I replied.

'Whether or not it fits is something I wish to come to in a moment.'

Laughter from the gallery.

'Members of the public should try to restrain their natural impulses,' said the Lord Chief Justice, who now seemed willing to take a more active part in the trial. 'Everyone present will be required to exercise concentration and sit patiently throughout what may become a very long and disagreeable case.' He shifted back into his robes, but no sooner had Mr Lemmons stood up to continue than he spoke again. 'And counsel must use terms that are familiar to members of the Jury. Could he explain the meaning of the term "check pessary"?'

'It is the device otherwise known as the cervical cap, my Lord,' Mr Lemmons explained.

'Worn over the male organ?' the Lord Chief Justice enquired.

'The female.'

'Worn over the female organ?' said the Lord Chief Justice. 'Would that not prevent coition completely? That seems a most complete form of contraception.'

'The cervix is part of the female interior reproductive system, my Lord,' I said. 'It is the gateway to the womb. Thus, by occluding that gateway, pregnancy does not occur.'

Mr Patrick Brain stood up. 'If I may intervene, my Lord,' he said, 'the cervical cap is fitted to the cervix which is at the terminus of the vaginal canal.'

'Ah yes, the vagina,' the Lord Chief Justice said. 'Let us keep these proceedings in plain English, if possible.'

'Of course, my Lord,' Mr Lemmons said. 'I only wished Mrs Haldane to explain the workings of the check pessary, or cervical cap.'

'May I have that in the form of a question?' I asked.

Mr Lemmons pursed his lips and stared at the

ceiling. 'How does the check pessary work?'

'The check pessary,' I replied, 'is a small rubber cap which is accurately fixed around the base of the dome-like end of the neck of the womb, also called the cervix. In the centre of the cervix is the tiny gateway I spoke of.'

'I am somewhat perplexed by this notion of a gateway,' the Lord Chief Justice resumed doggedly.

'It is more in the nature of a canal, my Lord,' I said.

'The vaginal canal?'

'No, a different canal,' I said. 'Another one.'

'Another canal?'

'Yes, another, much smaller canal.'

The Lord Chief Justice frowned. 'A smaller canal within the larger,' he said.

'The cervical canal is a small opening in the cervix,' I said, 'which is at the end of the vaginal canal.'

'Is that the finish of it? If there is more we had better know now.'

'The distance from the opening of the vaginal orifice to the end of the vaginal canal and therefore the beginning of the cervical canal is generally about the length of the woman's own finger,' I explained, 'although some women are made with short fingers and long canals, just as some have long noses and short chins. Such women may find it difficult to use this method.'

'With long noses?' the Lord Chief Justice asked.

'With long canals.'

'I see.'

'The salient point is that once the cap is in place

the sperms are unable to gain admittance to the cervical canal, and thus unable to enter the womb. They are confined to the vagina, which can be conceived as a sort of waiting-room to the womb, where they die quite naturally.'

Mr Lemmons, who had remained standing, inclined his head respectfully. 'I am obliged to your Lordship,' he said. He turned to me. 'Does the cap fit loosely into the vagina?'

'It is loose in relation to the vagina, yes.'

'So does that not mean that the sperm, which you so lightly condemn to death, might be let in?'

'I do not condemn sperm to death,' I said a little hotly. 'Nature does that. In every ejaculation by the average man, Mr Lemmons, are between three and six million sperms. Even when coition leads to the fertilisation of the ovum, all but one of those three to six million sperms are, as you put it, condemned to death. In any subsequent ejaculation, when conception has already been achieved, all, without exception, are, as you put it, condemned to death. In any act of reckless self pollution…'

'Perhaps you wouldn't mind returning to the question?' Mr Lemmons interjected quickly. 'Might the sperm be let in?'

'Certainly not.'

'Not if the cap is loose?'

'It is loose in relation to the vagina, but the cap does not fit to the vagina, it fits to the cervix.'

'Tightly?'

'Tightly?'

'Does it fit tightly?'

'It adheres.'

'If it adheres tightly – for that is what I take your answer to mean, that it is not loose – to the point of preventing the ingress of sperm, does that not mean that any matter secreted by the womb would not be able to get out? That is, if this cap is gummed and stuck fast onto the cervix, would not the dirty secretions from the womb be stemmed back and cause inflammation or sepsis?'

'No.'

'Are you not having your cake and eating it?'

'No. If there is any matter to be secreted by the womb, over and above that which would fill the cap, it will tend to dislodge the cap. It is a simple matter of hydraulics.'

'How long should the cap be left in?'

'No more than a day or two.'

'Is it not possible that a poor woman might put it up herself and leave it there for weeks without taking it out and cleaning it?'

'It is possible, but unlikely.'

'Are you going to pass from that, Mr Lemmons?' asked the Lord Chief Justice. 'Because the witness said just now that the cap might be dislodged. If a woman did dislodge the cap, or if it were dislodged, and it were not retrieved, would there not be the danger of the cap floating off into the body or getting lost among the other organs?'

At this ridiculous suggestion Mr Brain rose to his feet once again. 'I believe I can help your Lordship. If that were the case, rubber is an inert material and it would simply decay naturally in the body. And of course, a new cap could easily be fitted.'

'So am I to understand that a particularly

promiscuous or forgetful woman,' the Lord Chief Justice asked, 'might get entirely filled up with rubber over the course of a few years?'

A drunken cry.

'No, that is not the case,' I said.

'Can you be sure?' the Lord Chief Justice asked, eyeing the gallery.

'The vagina is completely closed off from the other organs, except for the tiny… entryway of the cervical canal,' I said. 'The cap could not peregrinate elsewhere.'

'You have never had a case in which a cap went missing, and a woman came into your clinic, rather anxious, saying "I had it in me last night, or last week, but now it is utterly gone, and I don't know what to do?"'

'Never.'

His Lordship raised an eyebrow.

'Now, Mrs Haldane,' said Mr Lemmons, 'if we can return to our *moutons*. If a poor woman kept it there for weeks would it not get very filthy?'

'I do not recommend it be kept in place for a great length of time, quite the contrary. The cap should be placed in its position shortly before use, at any convenient time, such as when dressing in the evening before dinner. The next day it should be taken out, cleaned, and if desired, re-inserted.'

'But if it were left in,' Mr Lemmons persisted, 'and there is no saying how long a poor or stupid or thriftless woman might leave one in – she might go for weeks without dressing for dinner, or dressing for anything – would there not be severe danger of secretions being blocked up or dammed up and leading to all sorts of complications, from this retention of these disagreeable fluids. Gangrene, for example? Peritonitis?'

'I do not think so, no.'

'Well, we shall see. You are not a doctor, of course?'

'I am a Doctor of Science.'

'Not a medical doctor?'

'I have never claimed to be such.'

'Yet at the beginning of your books you put "Dr Amber Haldane". If I were a Doctor of anything – for instance a Doctor of Chinese, or cattle-farming – would I be justified in writing a book giving medical advice and putting only "by Dr Lemmons"? Or if I were a Doctor of German Philosophy?'

'I say quite clearly I am a Doctor of Science.'

'Well, I will leave that. Do you wish me to address you as Dr Haldane?'

'I insist on it.'

'Whatever you please. Do you get considerable orders of your books from dirty rubber shops?'

'I am not aware of the existence of any shops selling dirty rubber.'

'Low rubber shops, then.'

'I confess I have not seen any of these shops either.'

'Have you not seen in the windows of shops of this kind various rubber articles with your books next to them, and a hand pointing to your books saying "Get your Haldane books"?'

This was quite childish. 'Not being aware of such shops, it would seem evident that I have not.'

'And you have never received an order for books from such a shop?

'I am not a publisher.'

'Is the purpose of your books to stimulate erotic fancies?'

'Not at all. On the contrary, my aim is to free sex life from the darkness of dirty-mindedness and repression. Every heart desires a mate. Male and female seek their opposites, in bodies clean and beautiful as their own, but fashioned from different flesh. My purpose is to educate loving couples precisely to abjure the filth you speak of. I seek to provide a light in our racial darkness, to teach normal, healthy people the way to raise eugenically fit families.'

'Would it surprise you to learn that anyone had been stimulated by your work in this respect?'

'Greatly.'

'Greatly,' Mr Lemmons repeated, lingering over the word. Rapidly thumbing a book on his table, he found a marked page. 'What then is the purpose of passages such as the one found on page 114 of *Wedded Love* – I quote: "The half-swooning sense of flux which overtakes the spirit in that eternal moment at the apex of rapture sweeps into its flaming tides the essence of the man and the woman"? Is that not a description of orgasm?'

'That,' I said, 'is merely intended to convey, in a descriptive way, the racial feeling of two healthy people. Much better that than the prurient information young people might get from the gutter.'

'Or this, from the recent edition of *Birth Control Monthly*: "Because of their new sexual freedoms and general more healthy living the Dutch people have increased by four inches in recent years. Bully for the Dutch! They've got the hot stuff!"'

This time the gallery did not stint themselves. There was a shriek of unparalleled piercingness. The Lord Chief Justice rapped his bench. One woman, who had something in her mouth, took the report of the gavel as a command to stop chewing, which, as she was also trying to stop laughing, produced rather an ugly picture.

'That is a piece by the noted American birth control campaigner Margaret Sanger,' I said when the hubbub had subsided. 'I did not write it.'

'But you agree with it?'

'I do not know. I have not measured the height of Dutch people.'

'I mean, you agree with her sentiments?'

'I neither agree nor disagree. It is her opinion. I was not aware that it is illegal to hold opinions on people's dimensions.'

'Do you conduct experiments on the poor?'

'I do not.'

'What is your campaign of birth control if it is not an experiment?'

'Birth control has been used for thousands of years.'

'Is it natural?'

'Are wigs natural?'

At this, in the manner of a man who, having swum long upriver, at last lets the current carry him out to the sea of truth, Mr Lemmons seemed finally to limpen.[12]

However, the Lord Chief Justice Mummery was ready with a final interjection.

---

12 The word 'limpen' is not in my copy of the Oxford English Dictionary, but it is so useful that I really cannot see why not.

'If you have concluded, Mr Lemmons,' he said in a manner that must have seemed to his junior overly vivacious, 'I wondered if I might ask something further on that question of thousands of years. Dr Haldane, you are a student of geology, I believe.'

'I am.'

'Then you know that the earth has been in existence for many thousands, millions of years.'

'About four billion.'

'Does it not occur to you that in all those billions, it has never been felt necessary to open a clinic such as your own, and that people have kept this business to themselves?'

The picture evoked, of solicitors, barristers and judges patiently plying their trade as far back as the Eocene, was a momentarily arresting one.

'It is perhaps because of the advance of civilisation, my Lord, in which people are pent up in stuffy cities, and all sense of natural life and sex life has grown dim, that we need more information on how rational beings should regulate their own fertility.'

'But could not mothers give this information to their daughters in a much more discreet way?'

I considered my response, aware that it would probably be my last utterance as a witness.

'Mothers, in my experience, rarely know much,' I said.

II

TUESDAY

I gazed out of the window of the office at the lawns of Westbury, where I could see a solitary bird-bath trembling in the haze.

'Our marriage is a byword for happiness,' I read. 'My husband is wonderfully loving and attentive to my every need. We have never felt the need for any kind of sexual relations.'

Throwing the letter aside (like a surprising number of letters I receive, the communication was neither signed nor accompanied by a return address), I took up the next.

'Having married my wife in 1919,' it read, 'I found we were particularly well suited in sex relations. After a few years I decided to convert her to the no-corset approach, with special vitamins, eggs and Swedish exercises, etc., and our sex life dropped off dramatically. Bearing in mind the expense already incurred, should I convert her back?'

A strong urge to neglect my correspondents and take to the Yew Woods possessed me. The afternoon was appallingly hot. I fell to thinking, as I had many times already that day, of Dr Ellis's Japanese experiment. The peace of the island, the majestic flying of spume, etc, and the appealing quietism of the brilliantined young man, seemed, in the midst of all the flurry of the trial, more than ever enticing. I wondered if the brilliantined young man had received the recent gift of my collection *Love Songs for Young Lovers* – a volume in which I had attempted to express the changing moods of a generalised 'I' – now a man, now a woman – in thrall to the power of Love, and employing a technique of intense lyrical expression superimposed on a background of hard scientific fact.

I had not attended the court session that second day. It had been scheduled for the testimony of Nurse Hives, who, however efficient a nurse, was unlikely to contribute anything of any importance; and for that of Sir William Hunt Furze, a fellow at the Royal College of Surgeons, who had agreed to provide evidence on the complete safety and efficacy of the cervical cap. Since my own statistics showed that the failure rate of the cap was well below .005 per cent – which meant that of every 20,000 caps used, only one failure could be expected, invariably through some fault of the woman inserting it – and, moreover, since I had exhaustively explained its workings during my own evidence – I saw little point in being present.

My prison of paper and ink became intolerable. I yearned to leave the stuffiness of the house and melt into the green shimmer of the day. Images floated before me: of cool limbs outstretched in wood or meadow; the azure dome above; the liquid note of the thrush; the scent of wood garlic.

Stepping out of the side door, I made my way to the beckoning yews. I wanted urgently to take all my clothes off.

III

WEDNESDAY

Eliot was dressed in a charcoal suit with a Botticelli blue tie and carrying a malacca cane with a silver handle. Vivien Eliot was not present.

'Mr Eliot, are you an American citizen?' Mr Brain asked.

'Yes,' Eliot replied.

'Do you live in this country, and are you married to a British citizen?'

'Yes.'

'I believe you have a doctorate from Harvard, among other distinctions?'

'I have.'

'You are the author of numerous books, including *The Sacred Wood* and *The Waste Land*?'

'That is correct.'

'What is the nature of your connection with the Plaintiff?'

'She and I are friends.'

'Do you approve of her work?'

'Wholeheartedly.'

'I want to get some sense of the support Dr Haldane enjoys, not only amongst poor people and the medical profession, but among the educated and intellectual classes generally and those who think deeply about the future direction of our society. What... ah... do you consider to be the chief importance of Dr Haldane's work?'

'She serves to remind us of the facts of life.'

Eliot's responses dropped into a sepulchral silence.

The gallery was now no longer anything approaching full. The presence of the commanding figure of twentieth-century letters had failed to stimulate interest. His answers were at once solid, authoritative and entirely abstract.

'Would you care to expand?'

'We have forgotten that for every birth there is a death.'

'That is so…'

'Birth and death are intertwined. Sometimes they may be very hard to distinguish from one another.'

Mr Brain nodded condescendingly. 'I am sure many women would agree.'

'Speaking personally, once was enough,' Eliot added.

'Indeed. Indeed,' said Mr Brain, gazing at Eliot in mild alarm. 'Indeed. Now, Mr Eliot, do you support Dr Haldane's campaign for family limitation?'

'I support Dr Haldane unreservedly.'

'Why do you think it is so important?'

'Polyphiloprogenitiveness should cease to be considered a virtue. One must think of its total effect. It may be an imposition on others; those in close proximity, for example.'

'What do you mean by that word?' Mr Brain asked, his alarm now unconfined.

'Which one?'

'The one you mentioned just now… I cannot say it.'

'If you could give me an indication of which one, I should be glad to help.'

'Well, perhaps I will pass from that. Thank you. No further questions.'

'Mr Eliot – or should I call you Dr Eliot?' Mr Lemmons began.

'I beg your pardon?'

'I might call you Dr Eliot, might not I, since you are a Doctor of Letters?'

'Certainly.'

'But you do not pretend to any medical knowledge?'

'No.'

'Well, I will stick with Mr Eliot, then.'

'As you wish.'

Mr Lemmons smiled pleasantly. 'Mr Eliot, are you in favour of life?'

'It does not matter very much whether or not I am in favour of it.'

'But surely it matters very much, if Dr Haldane and her campaign get their way?'

'There will be a danger to life?' Eliot asked.

'That is so, is it not?'

'To the lives of those now living?'

'To future generations.'

'It seems odd to posit a danger to something that does not yet have existence,' Eliot said slowly. 'I would say that a danger to the dead is more conceivable than a danger to the unborn.'

'I do not follow,' Mr Lemmons said.

'Unlike the unborn, the dead have existed, and therefore have a species of reality. They may be remembered or forgotten, for example. Of course, the dead may sometimes be more alive not only than the unborn, but the presently living.'

'Well, this is getting rather metaphysical. Do you not feel that tinkering with birth control is an experiment?'

'Life consists very greatly of tinkering, it seems to me.'

'This new venture, of controlling birth on a large scale, is an experiment, though, would you not say?'

'You say it is new. I would doubt that. One seldom sees anything truly new.'

'Many would not agree, I think. Very well, let us leave that. May I ask you about your poetry? What is the meaning of' – he referred to a paper in front of him – 'the lines from section two of *The Waste Land*, "A Game of Chess": "You *are* a proper fool, I said./Well, if Albert won't leave you alone, there it is, I said,/What you get married for if you don't want children?"'

Eliot, in a manner which characteristically combined hesitancy with command, appeared to ponder. 'They mean: "You *are* a proper fool, I said./Well, if Albert won't leave you alone, there it is, I said,/What you get married for if you don't want children?"'

'You can say nothing about their meaning?'

'Generally speaking, I find the best guide to the meaning of a poem is the language it contains.'

'I confess,' remarked the Lord Chief Justice from his eyrie, 'I do not understand. Poetry, you say?'

Mr Lemmons turned to face the judges' bench. 'That was a quotation from Mr Eliot's poem, my Lord, *The Waste Land*, published a couple of years ago.' He turned back to Eliot. 'Perhaps Mr Eliot will be more forthcoming. Let us not say "meaning". Poetic intention, perhaps. What is the poetic intention behind the lines immediately preceding the passage I have just read: "I can't help it, she said, pulling a long face,/It's them pills I took, to bring it off, she said./(She's had five already, and nearly died of young George.)/The chemist said it would be all right, but I've never been the same."'

'Is that a pentameter?' the Lord Chief Justice asked.

Eliot leaned forward. 'It is a mixture of pentameters and hexameters, my Lord.'

'What was the poetic intention behind that?' put in Mr Lemmons quickly.

'Poetically, it was intended as an experiment, in verse drama; an attempt, as his Lordship has correctly identified, to use a loose mixture of pentameters, and also hexameters, but retaining some of the qualities of naturalistic speech.'

'Deuced clever,' the Lord Chief Justice said.

'I think you know what I mean, 'Mr Lemmons said impatiently. 'Its theme is abortion, is it not?'

'Partly.'

'The woman has been to an abortionist?'

'Yes.'

'Is that a suitable subject for poetry?'

'May I ask how this relates to the work of Dr Haldane?' Eliot asked. 'She is not, as far as I know, an abortionist. Neither does she recommend abortion.'

'I am asking you if abortion is a suitable subject for poetry.'

'Abortion is terrible. Death is terrible. Birth is terrible. Life is terrible.'

'And so poetry must be terrible?'

Eliot's features were solemn. 'Poetry is often terrible.'

H.G. appeared in voluminous yellow. He stood with hands in pockets, answering questions with careless ease, gazing at his questioner through half-closed lids, and with his chin tilted up.

'You are Mr Herbert George Wells, the author?' asked Mr Brain.

'Yes.'

'I am sure your work is well known to the court. You are the author of numerous romances, and popular books on science?'

'Yes.'

'What is your connection with the Plaintiff?'

'We are colleagues.'

'Are you a Vice President of the Society for Constructive Birth Control of which Dr Haldane is a former President?'

'I belong to a good many societies.'

'But you are the Vice President of that society.'

'Yes.'

'And is that society in existence for the purpose of making experiments on the poor?'

'I have never seen evidence of it.'

'What is your opinion of the cervical cap, or check pessary?'

'I take the word of Dr Haldane when she says it is an effective method. I have never tried it myself.'

'You do not think there is any danger in it?'

'It is a thing of soft rubber. It could, I suppose, asphyxiate, if placed over the mouth and nose.'

Laughter erupted from the gallery. H.G. had attracted a large crowd.

'Dr Wells, I mean Mr Wells, are you among those in the educated classes, writers and artists, who feel that Dr Haldane is making a valuable contribution to society?'

'I think so.'

'What precisely would you say is its value?'

'Her campaign is symptomatic of a defining characteristic of modern societies: their propensity to change. Dr Haldane is an engine of change. She is quite possibly the most important engine in this country at the moment.'

'The most important engine you say?'

'Yes.'

'Is the future development of society safe in the hands of such an… engine, do you think?'

'The future development of human beings on this planet will be determined by engines such as Dr Haldane.'

'I see,' said Mr Brain.

Mr Lemmons stood up and carefully shook the sleeves of his gown, rather as a man does after a haircut. 'Mr Wells,' he began, 'in her own testimony, Dr Haldane said that part of her purpose in opening her Mothers' Clinic was to redistribute patterns of birth to eliminate the "degenerate and defective sections of the population". How can you say all this is not an experiment?'

'Surely we are all being experimented on all the time.'

'I am not sure I agree. By whom exactly?'

'That is a large question. Perhaps the most concise answer would be "by experimenters".'

'That does not get us much further forward.'

'The experimenter may be a blind force of

nature or it may be an unseen intelligence. There are human experimenters too, separate, but in our midst, who animate what was previously inert, and mould it into new life. Perhaps they are often invisible.'

'I feel this is all somewhat extraneous. To whom do you refer?'

'Women.'

'Women.' The word seemed to tire Mr Lemmons. 'Are women invisible?'

'There are none visible on the Jury.'

H.G. pointed to that body, which was indeed composed entirely of males. Some of them were in fact quite young men, who, owing to the nature of some of the evidence, flamed on and off like beacons throughout the trial.

'I feel your answer is somewhat frivolous,' Mr Lemmons said.

'Possibly,' H.G. replied.

'You say Dr Haldane exemplifies the principle of change. May not change be for the worse?'

'Certainly: it often is.'

'Then may not the changes proposed by yourself and Dr Haldane in the Constructive Birth Control Society or whatever it is called be for the worse?'

'Possibly.'

'So you admit that your campaign may be entirely negative?'

'I admit the possibility.'

'Is it a large possibility?'

'I am afraid that is not a very good question.'

'You must leave that to me,' Mr Lemmons said smartly. 'Would you mind answering it?'

'Once one has admitted possibility, the only way to narrow things down is to speak of probability.'

'Well then, the probability?'

'Very small.'

Mr Lemmons, aware that he had blundered into a trap of his own making, attempted to recover.

'On what do you base that assertion?'

'Progress, as it is generally conceived, is chiefly a question of the increase of control. Control of birth is simply part of that phenomenon. The notion that in future we will control disease, ageing and death, and travel to the planets, yet leave the process of reproduction entirely uncontrolled, seems a highly improbable one. You might as well argue that we should not have houses to control our environment or clothes to keep us warm.'

'That seems to me an argument for inevitability rather than rightness,' Mr Lemmons ventured.

'It is simply an argument along the lines of the following, something I often say when speaking on this subject: if you are opposed to birth control, take off your clothes.'

Laughter: H.G. turned with a smile towards the gallery. I was interested to note that the shrieker's place had been taken by a man, possibly her husband, whose laugh was a single, barking, ejaculatory 'Ha!'

'Mr Wells,' said Mr Lemmons, with a smile that mingled indulgence and dismay, 'Let me say this. Let me put this to you. Might it not be disastrous to experiment with the population by removing the working classes?'

'Even if we concede that that is indeed Dr

Haldane's purpose, which I do not: why would it be disastrous?'

'Who would do the work?' Mr Lemmons asked.

'Is the only reason to retain them so that they can continue to slave for us?'

('No!' from a red-faced man with a flattish head.)

'Whatever the reason for their retention, I am asking you now about the practical result of their elimination. What would happen if the working classes were eliminated?'

'They would be replaced.'

'By whom?'

'The middle classes.'

('Ha!' from the gallery.)

'Is that not rather a ridiculous idea?'

'I do not think so. In such a scenario everyone would be of the middle class, sharing the same advantages and the same low birth rate. The upper class would atrophy and the working class be abolished.'

'Is that not a scenario for revolution?'

'Revolution is generally conceived of as the opposite: the removal of the middle class by the working class, not the removal of the working class by the middle class.'

'Yes…'

'One might categorise this alternative as being anti-revolution, or un-revolution.'

'I am not sure I recognise the distinction you are trying to make. I repeat, you and your society are revolutionaries, are you not?'

('Yes!' from the man with the flattish head.)

'One must be wary of being captured by words

such as revolution, evolution, de-evolution, and so on.'

'I am obliged to you for your advice. Let us leave it that you can conceive of social change on a very wide scale as a result of these policies.' Mr Lemmons touched his forehead delicately with the tips of two fingers. 'Have you read Dr Haldane's books?'

'Yes.'

'Do you think they are dirty books?'

'You disapprove of the discussion of sexual matters?'

'I am asking for your opinion.'

'I think you know my opinion: no.'

'You approve of a fully-sexed young girl of sixteen picking up a book like *Wedded Love* and reading descriptions of the male organ in tumescence and detumescence?'

'Certainly. What harm could it do her?'

Loud laughter.

'I suggest a great deal.'

'You suggest that the books be supplied to her only when she has no use for them?' H.G. asked.

'I suggest that they are not supplied to her at all.'

'I do not supply them; you must look elsewhere.'

'I intend to. Very well. No more questions.'

There was a rustle of red fabric. 'You do not seem to do very well against the poets, Mr Lemmons,' the Lord Chief Justice observed.

'I am obliged to your Lordship,' Mr Lemmons said.

IV

VERVAIN

Poetry that is able to speak to the race is never the creation solely of an individual poet, as Mr Eliot himself is often at pains to point out.[13] The poet merely attunes himself to the divine vibration that exists in a sphere remote from ordinary sense.

After all, what are we? Clay? No. We are immortal souls, clothed in this flesh for a time, only playing at being human. We will live again, as we have lived before. And humanity is not the last word of creation. There will be a future in which beings unrecognisable to us will walk the earth: gods and goddesses, our descendants, but so beautiful as to dazzle our bleared eyes, stepping forward into a future bright with laughter and promise.

(Which reminds me, that of the five dozen or so men in the courtroom that week, barely 2 per cent were even acceptable, eugenically speaking. At least 50 per cent of the male population of this country should be sterilised as ugly or unfit.)

The future race will be a race built on the ennobling power of pure emotion. The rapturous ones, the great thinkers, the great experiencers, these men and women are humanity's destiny, in comparison with which the men and women of today will seem like a scrabbling race of dwarves, barely able to comprehend the sparks of divinity within themselves.

13 See for example 'The Art of the Quite Unspeakably Difficult', *Criterion,* vii, No. 3.

Critics carp; it is best for the poet to preserve silence. My own rhythms are not yet fine enough or large enough for the greatest waves of divine thought to pass through me. In future, when the human instrument has evolved into unimagined resonance with the divine, through selective breeding and sterilisation, poetry will achieve its greatest triumphs.

Press interest in the trial continued to be intense.

On the evening of the third day I had an engagement at Magdalen College, Oxford, to deliver my Number Three lecture, entitled 'Natural Desire in Healthy Women', which was to be covered by all the dailies, and I hurriedly motored up as soon as the High Court session concluded. It was about half past five as I arrived, coming in from Headington via St Clements, and found Magdalen Bridge thronged with people.

The college porter informed me that as the result of a last-minute ban I was to be refused admittance. His precise words were that I might 'run the risk of arousing the students'. In a display cabinet the Vice-Chancellor had posted a statement to the effect that he would not countenance 'any public meeting of undergraduates addressed by any lady on any problems connected with any issue to do with sex or the birth rate, or any matter calculated to give any offence' (which was comprehensive). The undergraduates carried me off to Ruskin, outside the university jurisdiction, but even there I had to speak outside. As the sun dipped in aureate fire to the west, more than 800 people blocked the High, cutting off Longwall Street and causing noisy traffic jams. One woman gave birth in the ensuing confusion. At the conclusion of my address, a handsome young man rushed forward and presented me with an armful of camellias, mixed white and red in the significant proportions of five to one; I learned later that his name was Evelyn Waugh, a young novelist. There, I thought, is one of the golden ones, the new generation of freethinkers. Even if it was not my destiny to smash organised religion, I had at least ascended the mountain. It was such as he and his fellows who would carry on the fight. Never, never would they bow the knee to the Catholic Church.

The next morning I received a letter from Dr Ellis:

> Dear Dr Haldane,
>
> It was very good to receive your letter and enclosures. The brilliantined young man seems very taken with your book, *Love Songs for Young Lovers*, which he keeps ever-present in his waistcoat pocket. He sends you in return the paper I have enclosed here.
>
> There have been many changes since I last wrote to you. The first upheaval was the arrival of dear Margaret, who landed amid an electric storm in the last week of April. The combination of the loud concussions from above and Margaret's apparition from the ferry cabin, drawing herself up to her full height in the half-gloom, was enough to raise yelps of superstitious rapture among the small group of islanders which had gathered

to meet the boat. I must tell you that now, a month after her arrival, a small Margaret cult has developed, which Margaret, with her customary breeziness, does nothing to discourage, regarding it as an atavistic manifestation of Great Mother worship. She has now quite the most magnificent of the accommodations on our hill, constructed in her honour in the vernacular style, with a verandah, carved red-painted wooden crayfish, rooms divided by bark screens, and *tatami* mats. Offerings of fresh fruit and flowers are perennially strewn on the steps of the verandah. Margaret is accompanied by a young factotum, one Pammy, whose main task is to arrange for the import of the considerable quantities of beefsteak that the new Deity demands as her daily holocaust.

Soon afterwards, Wilhelm Reich made landfall on the island, having been somewhat delayed on the mainland, bringing the complement of our community up to six – almost as many as in pre-earthquake days. I was overjoyed at his arrival, and to see once more that shock of blond hair, which, together with his ruddy cheeks, conspires always to suggest that he has only that moment been released from suspension upside-down. The new accumulator he brought as his gift to the island was also a cause of great celebration. The local people helped drag it up from the jetty, and it is now housed in the orgonatorium, recently constructed from the shell of the Buddhist temple, where it sits next to the original accumulator. The orgonatorium at this time of year is most pleasant: very cool, sitting in its grove of trees, with moss-grown stepping stones leading up to a door covered in delicately flowered vines.

So we have four households here: Françoise and myself in the central dwelling with its view south towards the mainland; Margaret and Pammy on the north side of the hill near a small heath of cycads; Wilhelm and a native girl he requisitioned a few days after arriving, a little way to the east; and the brilliantined young man near to us on the brow of the hill.

We spend our time in writing and experimentation. Wilhelm, as ever, interests himself in the function of orgasm. His contention is that frequent sexual crisis has a generally beneficial effect, helping to ward off disease and infection, reduce signs of ageing, enhance creative ability, improve digestion, smooth wrinkling, prevent oedemas, cure jaundice, haemorrhoids, blindness, acne, insanity, epilepsy, delirium, tuberculosis, memory loss, paleness, pimples, and, in some cases, death. An interesting new idea he is currently developing concerns the inauguration of a 'World Orgasm Day', in which every inhabitant of the planet will be encouraged to reach sexual climax on exactly the same day, at exactly the same hour, minute and second. He suggests as a possible date the 1st of September 1939, his mother's birthday thirteen years hence, since it might take some time to organise. The benefits in terms of world peace and harmony are perhaps too obvious to be stated. A secondary effect, Wilhelm believes, would be to send out into space a pulse of pure energy which could serve as a means of communication with extraterrestrial civilisations: indeed, he argues, the production of such an 'orgonotic pulse' might be the qualification for joining an already-existing club of advanced cosmic intelligences. Françoise objected that hostile countries might agree to participate in the World Orgasm Day but in fact attack just at the moment when our armed forces were in the throes of collective sexual paroxysm. Wilhelm, however, had anticipated her and presented detailed proposals for international verification by a specially created League of Nations secretariat, the League Orgasm Verification Executive, or LOVE.

This week his main preoccupation is to observe tortoises mating. The fact that the tortoise is exceptionally long-lived makes its sexual activity of great interest. His method is to load as many tortoises as he can into the accumulators and leave them there overnight, then observe their arousal levels on awakening.

The weather here is very hot and wet. In the valleys the mossy banks are hung with luxuriant fern growth.

Our diet continues to improve: we now

have various delicacies, including green ice cream, resembling pistachio but flavoured with the best of the young tea leaves, which is irresistible in the heat. Small cakes known as *o-kashi* have recently made their appearance and we have even managed to obtain a supply of demitasse.

The brilliantined young man – ah – what of him? He withdraws more than ever into Japaneseness, into the spirit of old Japan known as *bushido*, so close to the European ideal of knightly chivalry. Its essence is rectitude, frugality, honour, love of the arts, and, in time of war, the indiscriminate slaughter of anything that stirs. Having said that, he still dresses in precisely the same way as he did when we first arrived: in a Jermyn Street suit, handmade shoes, spats, a chartreuse tie and pearl-grey hat in all weathers. His embrace of the way of *bu* is shown chiefly in his growing mastery of Japanese calligraphy, and the fact that he always takes a dagger into the accumulator.

We have all heard about your trial, and I hope that by the time you receive this letter it will have been brought to a satisfactory conclusion. The forces of history are on your side. Margaret and Françoise send their love, and Margaret wishes me to tell you that never again will women be forced to breed human lampreys and cowards who murder those who are willing to die for freedom rather than live in slavery. Dr Reich says the entire judicial process should be looked on and treated as a neurotic phenomenon. I can only echo their sentiments, and add that the fountain of truth can never be permanently dammed, and must eventually, if only through the smallest chink, find ecstatic release.

With the very best wishes and apologies for this long letter,

Your affectionate friend,

Havelock Ellis

Accompanying the letter was, in beautiful calligraphic script, a translation of my poem 'Vervain' into the Japanese language, as follows:

クマツヅラ

愛は、私に待つように言いました
これら桜草が咲き散る森で
あなたの甘い手触りのために

愛は、私にとどまるように言いました
そして、長い日を過ごし
ここ緑柱石の陰で

それから玉髄の面ざしとともにあなたは来ました
そして、琥珀の髪
そして、薔薇色の処女の唇

そして、クマツヅラの舌を私の口に、
小さな哺乳類のように
柔らかな地のうえで

あなたの細波をたてる舌
皮膚、髪、そして胸のうえに
脈うつ生命によせて

紫水晶の火のような情熱
喜びにはち切れそうな私の感覚が
応えています

あなたの内なる生命の喜びに。
それから不意にあなたは旅立ちました
私をケシの花波に独り残して

この上なく満たされ
そしてさらに、恥じらうことなく燃えて
そして、あなたが戻り来るのを待っているのです。

V

THURSDAY

'Gentlemen of the Jury' (Mr Lemmons began), 'we have learned that Dr Haldane has many eminent friends in the world of letters. Dr Haldane is herself highly qualified. She is an expert in minerals, and coals, and so on. But I have noticed one thing rather missing from her list of qualifications, and rather missing from the list of the qualifications of the eminent witnesses she chose to testify as to her character and her campaign. They were none of them, or very nearly none of them, doctors. Dr Haldane is not a doctor in the medical sense. Mr Eliot is not a doctor in the medical sense. Mr Wells is not a doctor, in any sense. Contrast this with the situation and status of the Defendant in this case, that of Monsignor Dr Isidore Blackwell Garnet, from whom you will be hearing in a moment. He *is* a doctor. He is not only a medical doctor, but a practising gynaecologist. He is not a writer or a seer or a prophet. He does not look into the future and see it populated by gigantic land-crabs. He does not write poetry about abortions. He is a doctor, and he says that birth control is an experiment – he goes further, he says it is a monstrous experiment on the bodies of poor women.'

Mr Lemmons paused, resting his knuckles lightly on the table.

'Now, what do they find, these poor women, when they enter this clinic? Who is it that they encounter first? Why, Nurse Hives. Nurse Hives examines them. Would you, gentlemen of the Jury, like to be examined by Nurse Hives? Is she qualified to detect disease? Is she qualified to perceive the warning signs, to discriminate between the various discharges and venereal suppurations that constitute the various conditions of the womb, the cervix, the vagina, and all of that? She is not. The best she can do is to supply these sordid little rubber caps – the most harmful form of contraception known to medical science, as witnesses will corroborate – purely by dint of the fact that on a good day she has the main strength to push one up anyone who asks for it. She would in all likelihood do her level best to push one up any one of you gentlemen if you asked her. Nurse Hives pushes first and asks questions later. Are they married, these patients? They are married if they say so. It is all positively Polynesian.

'But this real doctor, the Defendant, Monsignor Dr Isidore Blackwell Garnet, has stepped forward, to his infinite credit, to criticise this campaign. This is his right. He wishes to ask questions. He does not care a button for Dr Haldane, or Mr Eliot, or Mr Wells, or for giant ants in gleaming towers of emerald. He cares only about the campaign and its potential evils. He cares about the bodies of poor women. He cares to do something against this monstrous campaign of birth control.

'Let us look at that campaign. Now, I appeal to the Jury as men of the world. Most of you know about the shops where these appliances are sold. You have seen them. You have passed by them in side streets. This is a fact of life. Rubber shops. *Oh, Mrs Haldane's shops are a different affair entirely*, her counsel will tell you. *Mrs Haldane is concerned only for the needs of married people and the health of society.* Criminal nonsense! I hope I may say this without the risk of losing the friendship of someone whose friendship I value, my learned friend – evil nonsense! What business is Dr Haldane in, if it is not the same business? She is in the rubber business, just as much as any rubber shop proprietor! She does not want clean and pure relations between the sexes. She wants ceaseless opportunities for fornication! Ask yourself what would happen if everyone became an adherent of Amber Haldane. What if every young woman, pure in heart, not yet married, were seduced into the abominable practice of birth control? What of the increase in fornication? In immorality? In the debasement of family life? In the destruction of all that we hold most dear? It is monstrous. It is an experiment.

'Yet this is only a part of it. The campaign does not end here. There is the matter of her books, from which Dr Haldane receives, as she says, a small income. It is an income small enough, or large enough, to maintain an estate in the country, with at least one cow. They must be very profitable, these books. What do they contain? Intimate, stimulating descriptions of the male and female organs in states of excitement; obscene delineations of exactly what goes where during of the act of copulation, that she and her supporters and counsel – who, if I am not imperilling my friendship with him, is either grossly deluded or downright venal – think is suitable reading for young ladies or children. Pages which tell of the fine aesthetic value of sexual crisis for young ladies.

'My learned friend has presented to you a woman fired by a noble cause and concerned for the poor. I beg to disagree, at the risk of making him out to be a dupe and a simpleton. I present to you instead a woman who wishes to sweep away thousands of years of common sense regarding sexual relations and install in its place a new gospel in which obscenity is put at the very heart of our civilisation as the supreme public good. This is the devilish gospel of Amber Haldane, which the young and impressionable are taught to admire: immorality, disease, pornography, degeneracy. National and racial suicide.

'With these observations, let us hear what the witnesses for the Defendant have to say. After you have heard them I do not think you will have much difficulty deciding upon the verdict you ought to give. I call Monsignor Dr Isidore Blackwell Garnet.'

Such was Mr Lemmons' opening speech, beginning, as it did, the second half of the trial. As an exercise in malice and misinformation, it was hard to fault. One is of course quite accustomed to being slandered, especially during trials for libel. But the familiar accusations of immorality seemed, even in Mr Lemmons' capable hands, a little weary. If I am immoral, are not shop windows immoral? Or cinemas? Or spring mornings and summer afternoons?

I fancy the Prosecution had done rather better, especially where it came to my own testimony. My evidence had surely done a great deal to educate the officers of the court and the Jury about the realities of the female reproductive system. In my long experience of litigation I have often felt that trials, whatever their outcome, are important for this very reason, if no other.

Monsignor Garnet now walked to the stand. He was not an attractive man. His nose particularly appalled me: it looked like a piece of clay that had once been a nose, but had been rejected by a sculptor and trodden on.

'Monsignor Dr Isidore Blackwell Garnet,' his counsel said with a flourish of his gown-sleeves. 'You are a Doctor of Medicine with Honours of Edinburgh University?'

'I am,' Monsignor Garnet replied.

'Do you hold the following position: Gynaecological Observer at the Convent of the Sacred Heart, Edinburgh?

'Yes.'

'And you have in the past been Chief Medical Officer of the General Infirmary for the Paralytic, Glasgow?'

'Yes.'

'That involved substantial caseloads, I believe?'

'It did indeed.'

'When did you first become aware of the Plaintiff's work?'

'I became aware of it around the time of the publication of *Wedded Love*, in 1918, as did many people in this country.'

'Was your distaste first excited at that point?'

'It would be fair to say that, yes.'

'What were your feelings at the time you wrote the review in the *Catholic Inquirer*?'

'My distaste was quite well developed by that time.'

'I can quite understand how it would have been,' Mr Lemmons said.

'As was the distaste of many of my friends and colleagues. So I wrote the review to do something about it.'

'Good. Well, that is clear. Now let us turn our attention to the paragraph complained of, in which you claim that the Plaintiff is guilty of an experiment on the poor. What did you mean by this?'

'I meant that she is guilty of trying to redistribute the birth rate contrary to the law of nature and the law of God.'

'You feel that the consequences of this experiment are unpredictable, because untried?'

'Yes.'

'You mention in the passage complained of that the check pessary is the most harmful method of which you have experience. What is your evidence for that?'

'It is well known among medical men and priests, and those who are both, that this form of contraception can lead to all sorts of gynaecological problems.'

'Is it the case in your opinion that the mere insertion of the pessary can prove dangerous?'

'Yes, certainly. If a woman scratched herself internally during its insertion, that could lead to infection.'

'Sepsis?'

'Certainly.'

'Inflammation?'

'Yes.'

'Gangrene?'

'Not impossible. All of these could follow if a dirty finger were employed. Any woman who touches herself in this area for whatever reason is running the risk of developing gangrene.'

'Might the gangrene be severe?'

'If by that you mean, might it be malignant, rapidly-spreading gangrene, life-endangering gangrene – yes, quite possibly.'

'Thank you,' Mr Lemmons said. 'Now, in addition to the remarks complained of, you believe, do you not, that contraceptives in general are likely to lead to intellectual and moral anarchy, that they make adultery more possible, that their use is on a par morally with the behaviour of, say, the Empress Catherine of Russia, for example? That is, in addition to their contra-indications for general health, the possibility of sepsis, inflammation, and so on, and the fact that stupid women are liable to forget these rubber devices are there altogether and let them rot and putrefy in the body? Would this be a fair summary of your opinions?'

'It would.'

Mr Patrick Brain stood up for the cross-examination.

'Doctor Reverend…' he began.

'Monsignor Doctor.'

'Monsignor Doctor, I beg your pardon. You have written that you find the works of Dr Haldane to be debasing, pernicious, degrading, etc – I choose at random from a large number of adjectives of this type – but do not you feel that even if all that *were* the case – and I do not admit for a moment that it *were* – I mean that it is – can you not see that these works are simply an attempt to try to teach people more about the realities of their own bodies in the least unpalatable way?'

'No. The indiscriminate broadcasting of this sort of information is extremely dangerous. What if an innocent child were to get hold of these books?'

'You object to children being taught about the facts of life?'

'In this way, yes, I most certainly do.'

'How then are they to learn?'

'Well, first they might be allowed to see earthworms.'

There was laughter, but the pugnacious set of Monsignor Garnet's chin showed that he was quite ready to defend the proposal.

'Earthworms?'

'Yes. Then perhaps a hen hatching eggs. After that, just before marriage, they might be allowed to keep rabbits.'

'You recommend earthworms?' Mr Brain repeated.

'If two earthworms are put together, they naturally writhe around each other.'

'And that is sufficient instruction?'

'To a receptive and enquiring mind that says everything that needs to be said. It also has the advantage that earthworms, having no limbs and no mammalian characteristics, are unlikely to exert a harmful and suggestive influence on innocents. I know of many convents which have wormeries for the instruction of nuns. They derive no information from them whatever.'

'Let us set that aside for a moment... I want to

look at the situation of an already married couple, one that is already familiar with… ah… connubial relations. Is there not some merit in the notion that they should be supplied with information to help them in their married life? To ensure they are happy together?'

'Not at all. This is simply pornography. After they're married, that should be the end of it.'

'What if they need some instruction as to how to limit their family?'

'I am utterly opposed to any such thing. D'you think I wear this sash for the good of my health?' He pointed to the violet sash that was draped diagonally from his shoulder, partially occluding his black cassock.

'Your sash has not escaped my notice, Father Monsignor Garnet; I am merely asking what you would advise a couple to do, who have already a large family, and do not wish to have further children. What are they to do?'

'Practise abstinence.'

'Do you really put abstinence forward? Are not strains and stresses likely to develop in such marriages?'

'Do you know a marriage without stresses and strains? What about a bit of backbone? Continence! It is essential in marriage! During pregnancy, for example, or three months after pregnancy, or on certain days in the liturgical year. To indulge in copulation during these periods would invite divine displeasure of the most strident variety, believe you me.'

Mr Brain seemed about to concur, but stopped

himself just in time. 'Do you agree with Father Xavier St John Montevergine when he says "I find much to commend in your writing," referring, of course, to the book *Wedded Love* by Dr Haldane?'

'Father Xavier no longer speaks for the Catholic Church. I am very much afraid that Father Xavier made a serious misjudgment.'

'What has happened to Father Xavier?'

'I am afraid I am unable to comment on that matter.'

Mr Justice Mummery raised two fingers in interjection. 'Yes, that does seem rather outside the bounds of this enquiry, Mr Brain.'

'I only ask, my Lord, because of the discovery of the body on Monday near Aylesbury, with the thermos flask marked "XSM".'

'That is *sub judice*,' the Lord Chief Justice replied shortly.

'Very well,' said Mr Brain, after a minuscule pause. 'Father… Doctor Garnet… Doctor Reverend Garnet. Why did you choose to describe Dr Haldane as a Doctor of German Philosophy?'

'I was simply trying to draw attention to her highest qualification.'

'You did not wish to convey that she was a German charlatan?'

'No.'

'You do not seek to tar her with the German brush?'

'No.'

'You are quite sure?'

'Yes.'

'Very well. No more questions.'

VI

FRIDAY

I had often thought of Mr Gandhi and his promise to send me something for *Birth Control Monthly*. The fact that he had reneged on this promise – as well as the fact that his general behaviour had been distinctly odd during our telephone conversation – only confirmed my suspicions that he was suffering from some sort of mental instability, possibly brought on by celibate religious practices.

Mr Gandhi, I was rather amazed to discover, was still in London, fully eight months since I had telephoned him at the Carlton. It was not perhaps his presence in London *per se* that was the cause of my amazement, but rather his exact whereabouts in London: in Court Four of the Royal Courts of Justice, as a witness for the Defence.

'You are Mohandas Karamchand Gandhi, also known as Mahatma Gandhi?' asked Mr Lemmons.

'Yes.'

'You trained at University College, London as a barrister and were admitted to the bar?'

'Yes.'

'Are you currently resident at the Carlton Hotel, London?'

'Yes.'

Mr Gandhi beamed. He seemed almost to bounce without moving. He was wearing a very smart suit with a pink tie.

'Let me see. I have it here that you served in the

South African army as a stretcher-bearer at the Battle of Spion Kop, for which you were decorated?'

'Yes.'

'Mr Gandhi, I have called you because I believe you can help us get a sense of the worldwide scope of this dangerous new idea of birth control. It is possible that one day its main application might be in the colonial sphere. The Plaintiff has already opened several clinics in parts of the Empire, including in your country. Her work is known to you, of course?'

'Oh yes. Dr Haldane and her campaign are very well known in India. She is very well respected.'

'What is your opinion on the matter of birth control?' asked Mr Lemmons.

'It seems highly inadvisable.'

'Can you say why?'

Mr Gandhi's face took on an expression of beatific reverie. 'You know,' he said, 'whenever a child is born into a Hindu family there is a celebration that lasts fifteen days. Guests are called. Huge quantities of sweetmeats are consumed. Then, one month after the birth, there is another celebration, this time lasting ten days. The guests are recalled. Comparable quantities of sweetmeats are consumed. This continues until the financial resources of the family are entirely exhausted.'

'What do you think would be the effect on the country if contraceptive measures were widespread?'

'Children would be less numerous.'

'And that, of course, would be bad for society, economic growth, and so on?'

'Ha ha ha ha ha ha ha! Very possibly.'

'Do you consider there would be an effect on morality?'

'People are moral because it is right to be moral. That is the essence of morality. That is fairly elementary, I think. Ha ha ha ha ha ha!' It was clear that the courtroom held few terrors for Mr Gandhi. 'However,' he continued, 'I feel that the theological aspect, perhaps more than the ethical aspect, is important here.'

'Could you elaborate?' asked Mr Lemmons.

'Any action to prevent the conception of a child would mean that there would be fewer bodies available to act as potential vehicles for transmigratory souls. We must surmise that if the birth rate of any nation is at a certain level, high or low, it is necessary that it stay at that level to provide bodies for the number of souls currently waiting to be reincarnated, as a result of previous deaths. Thus birth and death are intertwined.'

'Yes. I take that point, in the Indian religious context.'

'In any context. The law of *karma* is international in application. Ha ha ha ha ha ha ha ha ha ha ha ha ha!'

The gallery did not seem to know how to respond to Mr Gandhi's jokes, and remained silent.

'I defer to you on that. Very well. Now, are there any further reasons why you feel that contraception is generally a noxious influence?'

'Apart from the reasons already given, there is one further principal reason. The widespread availability of contraception would very probably lead to an increase in sexual enjoyment.'

'So fornication, and possibly adultery, would increase?'

'This is a technical point. Allow me to clarify. Attachment to sexual pleasure is an interposition between the devotee and God. Attachments to food or to material possessions have the same effect. It is not sexual enjoyment *per se* that is bad, you understand. It is just that it does not lead to happiness as efficiently as love of God. In fact it often leads to much misery. Ha ha ha ha ha ha ha ha! Ha ha ha ha ha ha ha ha!'

'I think I understand,' Mr Lemmons said. 'People who indulge in sexual pleasure without consequences are neglecting their religious and other duties and are putting pleasure before burdens and responsibilities.'

'That is perhaps an adequate Anglo-Saxon translation of the idea. Ha ha ha ha ha ha ha ha ha ha ha ha! Ha ha ha ha ha ha ha ha!'

'Thank you.'

Mr Patrick Brain stood up.

'Mr Mahatma Gandhi,' he said, 'you say that people are moral because it is right to be moral. Does that not mean that a young girl being seduced into sexual intercourse would not necessarily succumb, even if she were offered contraception? Would not her own innate sense of morality hold her back?'

Mr Gandhi rolled his head in appreciation. 'Yes, that is an excellent point. However, I was speaking of married couples. The existence of numerous children frustrates the desire of the husband and wife to be alone together, and therefore acts as a barrier to intimacy, you see.'

'I see,' said Mr Brain.

'But I agree with your point, certainly.'

'Thank you. Ah… Mr Gandhi, are you aware that part of this libel suit as it has been conducted so far concerns the wider campaign of Dr Haldane for sex education, as propounded in books such as *Wedded Love* and *Motherhood and its Enemies*?'

'I was not aware of that.'

'Have you read the Plaintiff's books?'

'I am afraid I have not. I rarely have time for reading. I have not read a newspaper for three years. I find them depressing. Ha ha ha ha ha ha ha ha ha ha ha ha ha ha ha ha! Ha ha ha ha ha ha ha ha ha ha! Ha ha ha ha ha ha ha ha!'

Mr Gandhi's laughter seemed to have a rather unnerving effect on Mr Brain.

'Quite. I do myself… but surely, Mr Gandhi, the frustration of desire you speak of – that is, within the sacrament of marriage – may lead to all sorts of problems?'

'I gave up sexual intercourse at the age of thirty-six, although I was still married. I am still married today. I remain celibate so that I can learn to love fully. I spent much of my youth in a constant ferment of lust. Ha ha ha ha ha ha ha ha ha ha ha ha ha! I spent many years battling against all sorts of lustful urges and fits of jealousy. They hardly left room for anything else. I was spending all my time pursuing sexual enjoyment! Ha ha ha ha ha ha ha ha ha ha ha ha ha ha ha! Ha ha ha ha ha ha ha ha ha ha!'

'So, in your view, it is not frustration of desire that causes problems, but fulfillment of desire?'

'Precisely.'

'I see.'

The name of Dr Anna-Louisa Mainprize will be familiar to many readers. A Professor of Obstetrics and Gynaecology at the Royal Free Hospital in Gray's Inn Road, she had been a frequent foe of the birth control movement since its earliest days.

In person Dr Mainprize is short, buxom and Caledonian. The engaging sweetness of her face – entirely misleading – finds its fullest expression in her lips, which have a remarkable sensuality. On that Friday morning in Court Four, as she took the witness stand, the gentlemen of the jury were seen to lean perceptibly forward, as if eager for whatever treasures those lips might drop.

'You are Dr Anna-Louisa Mainprize?' Mr Lemmons began.

'I am.'

'A Bachelor of Surgery and Doctor of Medicine?'

'Yes.'

'Have you had a very long experience in women's matters?'

'I have been a specialist in gynaecology since 1910.'

'Thank you. Now, I want to ask you about the rubber check pessary that is central to this case. It is your contention, I believe – one which is shared by Monsignor Dr Garnet – that the rubber check pessary is the most harmful method of contraception currently available. Could you explain why?'

'The check pessary cannot be inserted without a considerable manipulation of the sexual organs,' said Dr Mainprize, 'which I think is objectionable under any circumstance. Such manipulation actively invites sepsis, blood poisoning, endometritis, dysmenorrhoea, sterility, hyphaemia, vaginitis and many other conditions.' The list of diseases seemed eminently suited to Dr Mainprize's rolling Kelvinside diction. 'And that is before it has even been placed correctly over the cervix, which is by no means easy for anyone who is not a medical doctor. Even if successful placement has been achieved, the consequences of the occlusion of the neck of the womb which this necessarily involves are potentially very severe.'

'What are those consequences?'

'The possible consequences of prevention of the egress of the natural secretions of the womb, especially in a case where the womb is diseased, include inflammation, haemmorhage, chronic congestion, backache, abscesses, peritonitis, gangrene, and death.'

'Are there any other dangers,' asked Mr Lemmons, 'apart from sepsis, blood poisoning, endometritis, dysmenorrhoea, sterility, hyphaemia, vaginitis, inflammation, haemmorhage, chronic congestion, backache, abscesses, peritonitis, gangrene and death?

'Yes.'

'What?'

'Immorality.'

'Could you explain?'

'Fear of pregnancy, or the possibility of pregnancy, even among poorly educated people, leads to reluctance to become involved in sexual activity. Fear of disease has somewhat the same function. If fear, disgust, shame and guilt were all removed, or altogether divorced from, the sexual act, there would undoubtedly be an enormous explosion of all manner of immoral behaviour. Society would become almost unrecognisable. Moral values as we know them would cease to exist. The marriage bond and family life would be destroyed, and immorality would become not only permissible but the norm. One might say that society itself would become "permissive", if I may use that word.'

'It is new to my ears but I think it eminently descriptive. The "permissive" society.' Mr Lemmons paused. 'So, in the sense that widespread birth control might initiate unprecedented social change, do you consider that this campaign of Dr Haldane is "an experiment"?'

'Certainly.'

'What is your opinion of the writings of Dr Haldane, such as *Wedded Love* and *Motherhood and its Enemies*?'

'I think they also tend toward this end.'

'They are also an experiment?'

'Yes, they are highly irresponsible, and the cause of a vast amount of needless distress.'

Mr Brain rose.

'Dr Mainprize, your objection to the check pessary seems to be that it causes a series of rather distressing conditions,' he said. 'Do you really claim that it is difficult or impossible for a woman to insert one in herself without the possibility of sepsis, inflammation, vaginal gangrene and so on?'

'I do.'

'And that it can only ever be inserted safely by a medical practitioner?'

'If it were done by any untrained woman alone it could never be an aseptic procedure. As recommended by Dr Haldane it is septic from start to finish.'

'Why do you say that?'

'It is well-known that in all surgery you must have free drainage to prevent any trouble. Here you are absolutely contraverting that one main point of surgery. You are damming up the drainage, and you are damming it up with a dirty instrument.'

'Is this not a counsel of perfection?'

'Not at all. It is a counsel of good health.'

'Dr Haldane is quite clear that pessaries should be inspected to make sure they are clean before insertion, and that they should be kept safely – stored in a jar of water, I believe. Do you not think this is sufficient?'

Dr Mainprize compressed her superb lips. 'By no means. I am afraid this is wholly inadequate. There is no attempt at true asepsis. It is a dirty instrument. Any medical practitioner would tell you that as a minimum the pessary should be boiled beforehand, not kept in dirty water in a kitchen where cats might get at it. I should thoroughly boil it. I should then thoroughly wash my hands, scrubbing them with a nail brush in running water. I should put a rubber glove on the right hand. I should then proceed to pass the instrument up the vagina, having previously douched the vagina with some aseptic fluid, such as 1,000 perchloride. I should wear a cap and mask throughout, of course.'

'Well this rather brings us to the nub of it, does it not? My next question is not a pleasant thing for me, a man, to put to you, a woman, but I am afraid it is my duty. Let me ask you this… Take the case of a man who has connection with his wife – a working man, perhaps not a surgically clean one…'

Mr Brain hesitated painfully.

'His… ah… male organ goes, does it not, very much where your sterilised rubber glove must go for the purpose we have been talking about?'

'Certainly.'

'Is that correct?'

'Certainly.'

'Well, then… why is one more… ah… dirty than the other, in the sense that you have used the word?'

'Now I would say it is you yourself who are preaching a counsel of perfection. It is impractical for a working man to boil his penis before every act of coition.'

I have rarely seen a more amusing expression than that on the Lord Chief Justice's face at this remark. He had not, it seemed, expected to hear the word 'penis' in the witness's mouth.

'Yes, but I thought that was rather my point,' Mr Brain went on desperately.

'No, it is not, it is mine. I suggest only what is practical and possible to avoid disease. You seem to be suggesting a wholly unrealistic procedure.'

'I am mortified if you think I was suggesting anything of the sort. I quite agree that such an operation does sound extremely…' Mr Brain gulped.

'…impractical. My point, Dr Mainprize, is only this: if one, why not the other?'

'And my point, Mr Brain, is this: do what you can to help the patient. It is impossible to do more than one can.'

'I see,' said Mr Brain. 'Very well. I will pass from that. I want to take you on to your remarks about the Plaintiff's published work. Have you read the Plaintiff's books?'

'I have read *Wedded Love* and *Motherhood and its Enemies*.'

'You remarked to my learned friend that they were highly irresponsible, and the cause of an immense amount of needless distress. I put it to you that these books have been, on the contrary, a great help to many people around the world. Dr Haldane has received many, many letters from correspondents who have benefited enormously from the wisdom they convey. I want to ask you: what is your evidence that they have caused harm or distress?'

'I can recall cases of severe harm caused by the reading of books of a stimulating sex character.'

'But of Dr Haldane's works in particular?'

'Certainly.'

'What was the nature of these cases?'

'I recall one young woman of about seventeen who suffered from sleeplessness, wrecked nerves, and loss of health. She was nervous, jumpy and uncontrolled. I discovered she had read *Wedded Love*.'

To hear the chaste syllables of my book being pronounced as if they were *Five Nights in Baghdad* was annoying, to say the least.

'Do you mean to say that *Wedded Love* was the sole cause of all this?' Mr Brain asked.

'Yes.'

'How did this come to light?'

'I asked her: "Have you had a love affair or perhaps some other worry?" Bursting into tears, she told me that she had read *Wedded Love*; she could not get it out of her mind day or night; it had been such a horrible revelation to her.'

'A horrible revelation?'

'She had been brought up in a nice, clean home, and this is not a nice, clean book.'

'But you have heard Sir William Hunt-Furze and other eminent witnesses describe *Wedded Love* as entirely harmless, and likely greatly to benefit married couples and persons of all ranks. Sir William himself said that he thought Dr Haldane's book was, if I remember his exact words, "of intense interest". You do not agree?'

'No. It merely inflates a natural function like eating and drinking into a high art, like a gourmand with food. The book stimulates passion. This would perhaps not be so reprehensible among married people, but for it to fall into the hands of an innocent young girl is a disaster, a great disaster. A girl at that transition of life from girlhood to womanhood, when these dreadful things are most appalling. Horrible.'

'You do not think that this particular patient was neurotic?' Mr Brain tried hopelessly.

'It is hardly neurotic for a young woman to feel a natural revulsion from the male organ. As I say, she was a nice, modest girl from a clean home. If modesty and innocence are to be condemned as vices I certainly will not be in the vanguard of the movement against them.'

THE VERDICT

I have often observed that every social class has its own peculiar sex difficulty. *Ejaculatio praecox*, or premature ejaculation, for example, is perhaps the most common example of difficulty among our black-coated, or educated classes: doctors, professors, lawyers, judges, and so on. It seems that those who pursue a mode of life in which they are obliged to carry out their duties with the most meticulous and ponderous care sometimes find that in the arena of intimate relations they experience the most catastrophic and humiliating loss of control. Of course, this malady is the cause of real misery and is certainly no cause for scorn. Imagine a situation in which a typical sufferer weds an inexperienced younger woman. Imagine the feelings of that young girl on her wedding night. Full of romantic ideals, and glowing with the joy of her honeymoon, she gladly and lovingly gives herself to her mate, only to find that no sooner has she opened the gates of bliss to him than he soils the delicate fabrics of her nuptial garments in the most squalid and intemperate way. How else could she be expected to react, other than with disgust, loathing and hysteria, believing this degrading performance to be the precursor to a lifetime of married congress? Imagine her resultant eternal aversion to any idea of sex union!

I do not know why I mention it, except that such thoughts were idly running through my mind as I waited for the Lord Chief Justice to begin his summing up on that afternoon of the 26th of June.

The courtroom was highly agitated. A large number of journalists, Catholic apologists, etc., crowded the gallery. More waited outside with placards, straw hats, notebooks and cameras.

'Members of the Jury,' the Lord Chief Justice said at last, finishing with some paperwork and turning to that body of men as if he were surprised to find them in the courtroom, 'during the last five days, the microscope of enquiry has focused on all manner of matters generally left to specialists or else those with a morbid interest in sexual pathology and abnormality. But now we have come to that point of this trial when the focus shifts from these matters of disease, immorality and intimate acts, on to you, the Jury. It is your turn in the spotlight. Your function, like my own in this case, is to exercise absolute impartiality in arriving at a verdict in this matter of libel.'

The foreman of the Jury, a dull slab of a man, appeared to absorb the Lord Chief Justice's words. Impartiality, perhaps even insensibility, seemed well within his competence.

'Now, members of the Jury, it may be wise at this point to take some time to explain exactly what this impartiality means. You may have an opinion on what is called birth control; I may have an opinion. Indeed this is an issue on which there are profound differences of opinion. But our opinions, whatever they may be, have nothing to do with this case. We are here to decide instead whether any fair man, however prejudiced he may be, however exaggerated or obstinate his views, would have said what the

Defendant said in the alleged libel. If you decide that such is the case, and that what the Defendant said was both a sincere expression of his opinion and true to the best of his knowledge, then, however defamatory the words may have been, he must be acquitted. Perhaps our views may chime with his, that Dr Haldane is a generally evil influence on society, that her clinic is a monstrous experiment, that her methods are harmful. Perhaps they may not. However, this agreement or disagreement must not influence you in any way. Your own personal view that she is evil must not come into it.

'Now. Let us look a little more closely at the words complained of. The main allegations are twofold: that, firstly, Dr Haldane is in her work exposing the poor to experiment, and that, secondly, she habitually employs the most harmful method of contraception known to humankind, viz. the check pessary, or cervical cap.

'Much has hinged on this word "experiment". There is no suggestion that the Plaintiff is attempting to create a new race of men, perhaps a hybrid of men and lizards, or any such thing. The Defence considers the word "experiment" to refer to the whole campaign of birth control, the books, the proselytising, the ministrations of Nurse Hives, and the caps themselves. It is, the Defence contends, all one monstrous social experiment.

'As for the second allegation, that Dr Haldane habitually employs the most harmful method of contraception known: the Prosecution maintains that the check pessary, or cervical cap, has been used with complete success for millions of years.

You have heard other doctors saying that this is all wrong, that it may lead to gangrene, that it may lead to peritonitis. They say that if it is to do its work it must be fitted tightly, yet that if it is fitted tightly it might lead to all sorts of evils – evils connected with the secretion of matters that should descend from the womb through the cervix to the vagina, and all the rest of it. I have no doubt that you have the disagreeable thing quite present to your minds. That is what they say. The question that you must ask yourself is this: is this an opinion which they might fairly and honestly hold? Or all they all, to a man and woman, liars and scoundrels? If you believe the latter, you must convict. If not, you must acquit.

'You will shortly have two questions put to you. The first is, "Were the words complained of in this case libellous?", and the second, "If so, what damages should be awarded the Plaintiff?" Now it may be that the question of damages will not arise and the second question will not therefore be put. But if you should think – again, it is a matter entirely for your own good judgement and good sense – if you should think that in some slight respect what was written went a little too far, even though people like Dr Haldane who write books of this kind and publish them in this way must surely expect to receive severe punishment – if you think this, then damages might be awarded, though there is a very, very, *very* small coin of this realm which is sometimes thought suitable in such a case. But again, gentlemen of the Jury, let me repeat: the question is one entirely for you, and you will certainly not infer from the mere circumstances that I end upon the question of damages, anything in relation to their applicability in this matter.'

This was as fair a summation as I had been expecting from the Lord Chief Justice.

The Jury, led by the slabbish[14] man, now filed out. It was exactly four-thirty p.m.

H.G., who had been sitting by me that last day, began to eat an orange. Before he had quite finished, the Jury returned.

The twelve men sat down, and after a pause the Associate of the Court approached the Foreman, carrying a paper.

The Foreman stood up.

'Gentlemen of the Jury, are you all agreed?' the Associate asked.

'We are,' replied the Foreman, with a slabbish air.

'Were the words complained of in this case libellous?'

'No.'

There was immediate tumult: groans, cries, cheers and other noises, some seemingly not of any land animal. The man with the flattish head gave a shout of 'No!' Several people in the gallery rose to their feet and there were raucous cries of 'Guilty!' towards the back of the gallery. Since this part of the courtroom communicated, via a flight of stairs, to the hall of the main building, it was only a matter of seconds before the news passed outside, where the street was packed with people. Within a few seconds I heard a roar go up; it was difficult to say whether it was one of joy or lamentation, especially

---

14 I find to my surprise that 'slabbish' is not in the dictionary either.

since the word 'guilty', out of context, has very little meaning. There was a noise of something large falling over and a neigh of distress.

The reader will be able to guess at my emotions. Indignation, in which contempt vied with exasperation and a disagreeable sense of familiarity, were my overriding feelings. The Lord Chief Justice sat amid the clamour with very little expression. He seemed to be thinking about something else entirely, perhaps a personal trouble.

'In that case no question of damages arises,' he said finally, when there was a chance he would be heard. 'The Defence has made an application for costs.' He threw me a glance on the witness benches. 'I rule that they must be borne by the Plaintiff.'

A LETTER FROM THE NATIONAL GALLERY

Genoa has much to recommend it. It is the capital of the ancient Ligurians, and the name 'Genoa' is believed to be Ligurian for 'knee', because of the city's position at the crux formed by modern Italy and France. Alternatively it may derive from the name of the two-faced Roman god Janus.

From Genoa, the Blue Star line departs for Yokohama, by way of Ceylon, Singapore and Hong Kong.

This will be my second trip to Japan. I will not stay, of course. An appeal is underway. Meetings have already been held all over the country to protest the verdict. Fine, clean men and women have risen to speak out against the regressive forces ranged against me in that court.

The costs of the trial amounted to £21,325, 6s 7d, which included Defence costs of £19,022, 5s 2d. It emerged that the Defence had been paying Mr Gandhi's hotel bill since the action was brought in January. Mr Gandhi, it appeared, was very expensive. In order to keep him at the Carlton in the style to which he was accustomed, very large sums were disposed of for room service and personal valeting, as well as for such things as gifts, tips, spinning wheels, imported salt and aromatic unguents, etc. He also demanded an extravagant fee as an expert witness on Hindu cosmogony. Mr Lemmons too had been paid at a fantastic rate, his forensic skills having been proved in 1924 with an impressive win in the case of Concepcion vs Allied Butchers, in which a Catholic businessman resident in London, Raul Concepcion, had been accused of raiding and destroying butchers shops that sold hare-meat, long anathematised by the Catholic Church.[15]

Today I visited the Aquarium, reputedly the largest in Europe, and afterwards dined at my hotel in the Via Scarpanto. Later I wandered the ancient streets by moonlight, the last chance I shall have before the boat sails tomorrow. A few shops were still open, selling watches, toothbrushes, toys and an Italianate jumble of other things. Amongst their wares I saw a jar of lotion not unlike brilliantine, which, though naturally inferior in quality, I purchased as a light-hearted gift.

Returning to the hotel I received a telephone call from H.G.

'I have been approached by Adolf to write your biography,' he said.

'Yes.'

'I managed to complete most of it last Tuesday.'

'I see.'

'I am considering a number of titles. *You Can't Be Too Careful* is my current favourite. What I wanted to ask, to bring it up to date, was this: what do you feel was the ultimate outcome of the trial?'

15 See Deuteronomy 14.7 and the Epistle of Barnabas 10.6: 'Moreover thou shalt not eat the hare. Why so? Thou shalt not be found a corrupter of boys, nor shalt thou become like such persons; for the hare gaineth one passage in the body every year; for according to the number of years it lives it has just so many orifices.'

'You know as well as I do,' I said. 'I have had to sell Westbury. *Birth Control Monthly* has been discontinued.'

'Yes, I mean apart from that.'

'Apart from the fact that I am homeless and poor?'

'Yes.'

I paused. It is often wise to weigh one's answers with H.G., especially if he is engaged in writing one's biography. In fact it is wise to have complete control over the output of biographers at every stage.

'It will allow me to improve my Japanese,' I said finally.

I am looking forward to seeing Dr Reich again. I have a small package for him from Dr Harvard, consisting of two very small jars to be filled with certain fluids from the tortoises he is experimenting on: doubtless the fact that the tortoise is a very heavy and slow-moving animal, as well as an exceptionally long-lived one, have motivated this unusual request. I look forward also to seeing dear Margaret. How thrilled she will be to hear that her words have been fought over in a British court!

The brilliantined young man remains very much in my thoughts. I cannot help wondering how he liked my most recent gift, a copy of my new play, *The Rapture, or, Thoughts from a Yew Wood.*

As it happens I am also the bearer of good news for Dr Ellis. Shortly before leaving London I received a letter, unsigned, on cream laid paper, bearing the emblem of the National Gallery. It nestles now in my handbag. Alone in my hotel room, I retrieve it and hold it between my fingers. It reads as follows:

Dear Dr Haldane,

I am contacting you with some trepidation, since there is a small possibility that you may not be personally connected with this matter. However, given your well-known association with Dr Havelock Ellis, the writer, and your sole residence at Westbury Park, Dorking, I surmise that it must indeed have been yourself who signed the petition that we received from Dr Ellis some months ago, in September of last year.

There were in fact only four names on that petition: those of Dr Ellis, first; 'A. Wellwisher' from the estate of Westbury Park, Dorking, second, whom I presume (if you will forgive me) to have been yourself; Françoise Delisle, third; and Professor Eugen Keppel, fourth. Françoise Delisle and Dr Ellis I understand to be in Japan, although my researches have been unable to discover exactly where; Professor Keppel is, sadly, no longer with us; which leaves only yourself as a possible point of contact on the matter I wish to communicate to Dr Ellis. This matter is extremely sensitive and of the highest importance. If it would be possible for you to pass the information I am about to disclose to you to Dr Ellis, I would be most grateful. If you absolutely cannot, or are in fact, despite everything, entirely unconnected with this matter, I beg you to destroy this letter, preferably by burning, and not speak of it to anyone else.

You will remember the subject of the petition. Dr Ellis's suggestion was that the famous portrait 'Woman Bathing in a Stream' by Rembrandt van Rijn, acquired by the museum as part of the Holwell Carr Bequest of 1831, was an 'Undinistic study'. That is, it originally depicted a woman in the act of urination, but that the falling stream was, at some time in the painting's history, effaced for reasons of prudery. I was, at first, of course, inclined to dismiss this idea as ridiculous. But it so happens that one of my Assistant Keepers, reading the letter that accompanied the petition, said that he had once noticed, while watching the picture being cleaned, that the handling of the paint in this particular work was unusual, and that there was an area of impasto in exactly the place that would have been implicated had Dr Ellis's theory been correct.

As you may know, the model for the painting is very probably Hendrickje Stoffels, Rembrandt's housekeeper, who lived with Rembrandt as his mistress. The painting may have had an Old Testament subject, such as 'Susannah and the Elders', or 'David and Bathsheba', both of which involve older men spying on younger women in states of undress. The painting was never finished, and there is no evidence of a completed painting. It seems unlikely that it was a sketch for some larger work, since Rembrandt did not make initial sketches in oils. The work therefore is something of an oddment on several levels, and it was this element of mystery, as well as the quality of the paint, that persuaded me to have it looked at more closely.

You may have guessed by this point what was uncovered.

We at the National Gallery were, then, in November last year, presented with a rather difficult dilemma. Either restore the painting to its former state and face the consequences, which inevitably would have included its withdrawal from public gaze, or conceal the discovery and pretend it had never been made. Opinions were expressed forcefully on both sides. Soon, however, the matter was taken out of our hands.

A junior colleague with responsibility for the Rembrandt holdings, which number about twenty paintings, began to wonder whether this circumstance was unique in Rembrandt's work. His interest focused on one painting in particular, 'Saskia van Uylenburgh in Arcadian Costume', in which the model is holding an elaborate floral bouquet in front of her dress. The bouquet has been known since the early nineteenth century to be an addition, and is painted in a markedly different style from the rest of the work. My colleague brought this to my notice, and I decided – reluctantly – to investigate. What we found underneath the bouquet, emanating from the front of her dress in a generous arc, will perhaps fail to surprise you.

The entire Rembrandt collection was analysed. Among the paintings with telltale areas of impasto were: 'An Elderly Man as Saint Paul'; 'The Adoration of the Shepherds'; 'Anna and the Blind Tobit'; and 'The Woman Taken in Adultery'.

It was at this point that I returned to Dr Ellis's letter; I urgently needed his address. On reading it again, I discovered that Dr Ellis had not only mentioned some of these other Rembrandt works which we had ourselves independently identified as possible 'Undinistic' candidates, but had actively suggested that similar preoccupations might be concealed in paintings by Piero, Caravaggio and Vermeer, all of whom are, as you know, well represented at the Gallery. By this time we were inclined to take Dr Ellis's prognostications very seriously, and these works too were thoroughly investigated.

The results were, in many cases, positive – if I may use that word.

If only from an art-historical point of view, I hope, Dr Haldane, that you will appreciate the immense significance of these discoveries. I also hope that you will recognise the importance, at this stage, of keeping the matter entirely secret. This letter cannot be signed. It is for Dr Ellis's satisfaction only. If he takes it to the press, which I am sure as a gentleman he would not, I regret to say that I and the Trustees of the National Gallery would deny everything. This letter is solely an expression of gratitude to Dr Ellis for this extraordinary new insight into the work of the greatest masters of Western art; an insight that will, one day, when public mores are rather different, be revealed to an astonished nation.

With many thanks for your assistance,

Yours sincerely,

The National Gallery 'U' Group.

Rebirth
by H. G. Wells

If this story is to be credited, it was all the fault of a
folding bed. And if it is not to be credited, there is
the question of witnesses – witnesses of the highest
calibre, including a man of the cloth. There is also
the Biblical precedent: I point readers in the direction of John 3:1–15. But frankly, I count myself
among the sceptics.

Perhaps it is best simply to lay the facts of the case
before the reader and let him decide for himself.

I had called on F--- several times that October,
hoping to find him at home. It was a matter of a
small debt for a picture I had sold him. My situation was becoming more and more tenuous. I was
beginning to come to the conclusion – in fact, I *had*
come to the conclusion – that I should be forced to
give up my dreams of painting: my resources, both
financial and artistic, were at an end. Ten months
ago, I had begun boldly enough, with a display
of powerful new ideas in a manner I dubbed (to
myself) Diagnostic Fauvism, but had not sold a
single canvas; I toned down the more immediately
shocking aspects of my style, and sold one painting,
but only one; I made yet more concessions, and
began to have a pitiful dribble of sales; and I threw
out all painterly ambition altogether, and produced
only what I thought would sell, and for a time made
enough to live from hand to mouth in a wretched

room in Clerkenwell, with a patent-medicine sales-man over me and a begging-letter writer below me. But winter was fast approaching and I had nothing left over for coal. Debtors I could certainly not afford. And so, having a debtor in F---, I made concerted efforts to find him at home and recoup my eight shillings.

It was a Thursday evening around the middle of the month, about six o'clock, and a lamp was already burning in the street outside F---'s house. A very fat maid answered my knock at the door. This was encouraging. Not her fatness; her fatness was neither encouraging nor discouraging. What was encouraging was the fact that in the previous week there had been no response at all.

'Is Mr F--- at home?'

'Yes sir. Who shall I say?'

'Mr Holland.'

'Just one moment, sir.'

The woman left me outside in the cold rather than showing me into the parlour, but even so, it looked very promising. I felt sure now of getting my eight shillings. Even if by some chance F--- was temporarily short of cash, I would make an ap-pointment to see him the following day and settle the matter then. I would, if necessary, press the point. It was wanted immediately.

I soon saw his small figure through the door-glass, bounding along the hall. To another it would perhaps have looked like a silhouette of a child, but I knew it was F---.

'Holland! Come in!'

'Hullo F---! Not disturbing you am I?'

'Not at all, my dear fellow! Let me take your coat! I was expecting you all last week!'

That rang a little oddly. I had called two days previously, and two days before that, and the day before that, and found all the lights on inside, but received no answer.

'Come into the smoking-room,' said F---. 'You must be frozen. Come and have a drink. And I want to settle up for the painting. I'm so sorry it's taken me so long – I've been most awfully busy.'

'Oh, don't trouble,' I said. The delicious prospect of a whisky and eight shillings made me lightheaded enough to risk this small display of carelessness. And, as I had expected, F--- insisted once more that I should have the money. He led the way down the hall into the smoking-room, and I followed him, thinking to myself what an extraordinarily little man he was – quite minuscule. He did not have the physiognomy of the dwarf – large head, stocky body, no neck – but was proportioned very finely, perhaps even more slenderly than average, with delicate tiny wrists, childish hands and feet, a small but shapely neck and head, and a narrow face with a pointed chin. The heels on his shoes were rather thick, and had doubtless been specially built up.

'Have a seat,' said F--- as we entered his retreat. 'Cigar?'

'Thank you, I will.'

I cut the end and lit a spill from the fire. F--- did likewise, and we were soon both puffing away. F--- took a decanter from a septagonal table near the hearth rug, and poured two whiskies. The room was warm and extremely agreeable, and only the sight of my painting on the wall near the lamp intruded on my sense of well-being. Comfort, ease and alcohol always act on me in such a way as to re-kindle ambition, but the painting reminded me that it was all up with me. It was a shabby thing, this product of my latest phase of artistic degeneration. Yet F--- obviously liked it well enough.

'You've been working on some experiment, no doubt,' I said. My friend was a chemist. 'I thought perhaps you'd gone away.'

He looked at me closely. 'Not really,' he said. 'That is, I have, but…' He gave a queer sort of laugh, evidently aware that explanation would have to follow. 'I have been through rather a time in the last week. You are almost the first person I have spoken to in seven days. Except…' His eyes drifted to the door.

'The maid?'

'Yes. Did you notice her?'

'I did.'

'Did you notice anything about her – physically?'

'Not particularly. A rather large young person.'

'Exceptionally, I think. I would say she is well over twenty-five stone. Perhaps as much as thirty.'

'Yes,' I said, thinking. 'Yes – quite possibly. Must take a lot of feeding.'

'She and I are engaged to be married.'

I did not blurt out my astonishment there and then, I think. But it was some time before I was able to recall that the proper thing to say in such circumstances was 'Congratulations'. I said it.

'Thank you, my dear fellow.'

I looked at him for signs of jubilation. There

were none. The warmth of the room had not produced any answering glow in his cheeks; his thin little face was very white, so white it might have been bleached. His thin lips were colourless. He was wearing spectacles with horn-rims, and only his eyes gave his face any life; they were large and bluish-grey. I hoped he was not going to ask me to be his best man.

'We have been engaged exactly one week. I proposed to her – if you wish to call it that – last Thursday evening. The solitary nature of my work and the fact that we are constantly together – she has a room downstairs – made it inevitable, I suppose. She has no one. I have no one. But it's a difficult business all the same. It won't affect my career – it's not in the nature of chemists to be particularly interested in the marital habits of other chemists – but everyone else will get hold of it, and she may be upset. They'll worry it like a dog with a bone.'

'Oh, don't worry about other people,' I said. 'You must grab your happiness while you can.'

'Yes,' he said, savouring the platitude without any visible irony. 'But I feel I ought to tell you something else. I must tell someone. It is barely credible.' He picked up the decanter and with a faltering hand poured himself a second glass. He then refilled my own. This slight lapse of etiquette was enough to impress on me that something was perturbing him.

'Now, Holland,' he proceeded, hesitating between his words, 'You are a broad-minded fellow. You are not the sort to condemn a chap because he wants to marry his maid.' He took a gulp of his whisky. 'And I know you've had your own romantic adventures. Don't deny it. You told me yourself. There was… well, I won't mention any names. A certain person. I know it's not my business to bring such things up – that's your affair. I certainly make no judgements. I was flattered at the time that you wanted to confide in me. Perhaps a little astonished too, that you considered confiding in me, her brother. And, how shall I put it, someone such as myself, who obviously… who obviously is not very experienced with women. I was even a little shocked at the time.' He looked at me intensely for a moment. 'Still,' he continued, 'what I am about to tell you is perhaps even more shocking, I think you will be the first to say. Indeed it is more than shocking – it is amazing. It is grotesque. You see, we have lived as man and wife for some time now.'

'F---!' I said.

'Precisely.'

'You have told no one?'

'Not a soul. We were going to go on indefinitely, I believe, but then last week something happened which made that all impossible. Now, Holland, I will say again, you are a broad-minded chap, so don't be scandalised at what I am about to tell you.'

I could not imagine what F--- could say that could be more scandalising than what he had already told me.

'I cannot skirt around it,' he continued. 'It has to be told. You will think I am lying.' He again looked at me rather oddly, as if he were not sure whether to go on. The flames from the fireplace lit his tiny body, and his shadow ascended the wall and danced there. 'Well, whether you credit it or not, I must tell you. The facts are as follows. Myrtle and I were in her room. It was, as I have said, last Thursday evening, about six o'clock, exactly one week ago. We were – I must tell you – on the folding bed. It is a large and sturdily built cot bed that folds up with a spring. You release a lever and it snaps shut. Rather a nasty snap. I don't know why they make them like that. If you didn't know it you could hurt yourself with it. Anyway, we were both there. I wouldn't be telling you this if it were not important for what happened next.

'You are doubtless sensible of the fact – who could not be? – that we are very different in build, Myrtle and I. Now, Myrtle is, as you pointed out, a very large young woman. Beautiful, kind – but large, very large. I, on the other hand, am small. I don't pretend otherwise. I must look very odd to most people, I know. The juxtaposition of myself and Myrtle in any public place would be, to any observer, quite comical, I can see that. Of course we have never been out in public.

'At any rate, we were together on the folding bed. Now, the next point is critical. You will have to forgive me. It is a single bed, and I was in a position in relation to her person which is… rather delicate to describe. I cannot, even having gone this far, quite put it into words. But I will have to, I see. It is too closely germane to the issue. All right then, I will say it. My head was quite close to the crux of her lower limbs. I have said it. I had to say it. Well, then, having said it, I will continue.

'All right. Now, as I have told you, it is a folding

bed. The catch that releases the lower half of the bed is operated by a lever at the side, about three-quarters of the way down. I don't know how it happened, but I must have flicked it with my foot by mistake, because suddenly I was aware of a terrific force pushing me from behind. The bed had been set in motion and was intent on folding itself up. I am naturally quite light, of course. I was sent rocketing towards Myrtle with the most sickening violence. I could not stop myself. I had no time even to cry out. My head was propelled directly into her body.'

'My God!' I cried.

'Yes. I am afraid so. My head was, without warning, suddenly engulfed inside her, right up to the neck. I could see absolutely nothing. I was in terrible anguish, flailing with arms and legs to free myself. The Lord only knows how Myrtle felt. The bottom half of the bed had closed on us like some gigantic bivalve. It was absolutely immovable. The spring, having catapulted it over us, had locked it in place. A ratchet of some kind. Devilish contraption! We were stuck fast. At the seam, where the bed folded, my legs were sticking out at the sides. Myrtle's lower limbs too dangled out from the edge a little way up from mine, the entire bottom half of the bed now sealing us both in, with what had previously been the foot of the bed now resting just on Myrtle's chin.

'As you can imagine, I continued struggling to free myself, but had absolutely no purchase. I could not go back because the fold of the bed was blocking me. Myrtle could not move because the bed was pressing down on her. I could not paddle back with my legs because they did not reach the floor, and in any case I could never have moved the bed, which is extremely heavy, and certainly not with Myrtle's and my own combined weight upon it. We were completely, irremediably stuck. I expected to suffocate at any moment, but when I tried to breathe, found I could respire almost normally. The air was thick and hot, to be sure, but there was some source of oxygen. I soon realised what had happened. I had been wearing these spectacles, which you see. At the moment of crisis they had become trapped around the region of my neck. They were creating an opening just wide enough for air to pass in and out. Without them, I doubt if would be talking to you now.

'All this time Myrtle was making sounds quite audible to me in my extremity. They were long, shuddering, gasping moans, which, mediated through the great vibrating chamber of her torso, gave an impression not of pain, but of some completely different, unearthly emotion. I was, I suppose, relieved to hear that she was still alive and conscious.

'Then something else odd happened: I found that I could see. At first, of course, I was in total blackness, but as my eyes became gradually accustomed to the gloom, I saw a reddish glow in the walls of the cavern, and the lineaments of my surroundings began to emerge out of the darkness. The walls rose all around me, blood pulsing through capillaries beneath them; a great veined mass that I took to be the uterus was suspended over my head, dripping a sickly violet fluid. The protrusion of the cervix gaped at me, opening and closing slowly, making a slight sticky sound, like a dry mouth. I am no physiologist, still less a gynaecologist, but I know the basic facts. Below my chin, I presumed, was the epithelium. Further on was a transition zone where the tissue seemed to undergo a change, looking a darker, deeper Indian red; this was the so-called columnar epithelium, which also forms the tissue of the cervix proper. Where the cervix reached down, two passageways, as it seemed, went left and right – but on closer inspection these were revealed to be not passageways at all but vault-like recesses – the fornices, in fact, as I later learned. The walls, wherever I looked, were marked by the characteristic vaginal corrugations, and everything was sticky from the action of the mucin-secreting glands. The secretions were quite acid, but there was no discomfort to the face, only a tingling, like being immersed in mineral water.

'Well, now for the last, and most astonishing detail of all. We stayed like that for four and a half days. Neither of us could move during all that time. We neither ate, drank, talked nor moved. I think we occasionally slept. Myrtle periodically stopped making sounds, when sleeping I guessed, but she would recommence as soon as she woke up. And we stayed like that, unmoving, unmovable, until our rescuers arrived.'

'Your rescuers?'

'The boiler repairman. He was due on Monday morning. He had instructions to let himself in at the back. The door was unbolted. And the boiler, as we knew well, was in the basement adjacent to Myrtle's quarters. So – that Monday morning, after an eternity of waiting, we finally heard his footsteps descending the stairs. It must have been around nine o'clock. Myrtle straightway called out to him. I heard his footsteps approach the bed. One glance was enough. He immediately threw down his tools and rushed to help us, first of all releasing the bed from the ratchet and folding it back. He then gripped my shoulders and began to pull. Myrtle screamed loudly, and he desisted; but, seeing that that there was nothing else for it, he reapplied his grip and heaved again. I was afraid he would dislodge the spectacles and it would all be over, but I think he divined that they were doing a useful job in breaking the suction and allowing the passage of air, and left them in place. He is a singularly intelligent man. But despite sweating mightily, all the while accompanied by Myrtle's cries of labour, he could not budge me.

'At that moment there was a loud knock on the front door. The boiler-man, glad of the prospect of some assistance, ran to answer it. It was Father Nicodemus calling about the cathedral roof. The next moment the pair of them were clattering down the stairs and into the basement, the boiler-man giving Father Nicodemus a précis of the situation as they did so. Father Nicodemus too rapidly grasped our predicament, and, taking charge, instructed the boiler-man to take Myrtle tightly by the shoulders while he applied himself to my person, and then to pull in opposite directions. Father Nicodemus is a muscular man. With the very first heave of their combined strengths, and a great elastic convulsion from Myrtle herself as she bore down on my head, I was free.'

And there F---'s tale ended. I have given it in his own words.

After he had finished we both sat in silence for some time, watching the coals grow dim in the grate. The telling had been so earnest that I could not find it in my heart to ask for further explication of this point or that. There were certainly a number of questions in my mind. Why, for instance, could F--- or his companion not release the ratchet? Where was the release lever located? Was it truly possible that they had continued in such a state all that night, then the next day and night, then the entire weekend, until nine o'clock the following Monday? It seemed incredible.

I must have got up in a trance and, stumbling out some words of leave-taking, allowed F--- to show me to the door, because about half an hour after I had first called, I found myself outside in the street again, standing under the lamp, the air a little frostier and the night a little darker.

And still without my eight shillings.

'A BALLS-ACHINGLY FUNNY WRITER'
ROWAN PELLING, DAILY TELEGRAPH COLUMNIST

THE OXFORD DESPOILER

and other mysteries from the case book of Henry St Liver

GARY DEXTER